THE TEST

Pat is a daughter of immigrants and a teacher of immigrants. She has a daughter and a son from a marriage she left twenty years ago. More than a year ago she lost her mother, and she is still grieving with an intensity that surprises her, an intensity that magnifies pressures she feels from two sides: from her dependent, demanding eighty-year-old father and from the threat of AIDS facing her thirty-year-old son.

Today Pat must see her father through The Test, the final appeal in his struggle to keep his driver's license. For Pat, living this day is like putting together a jig-saw puzzle of a family photograph obscured by multiple exposures across the years. Words and objects in her parents' house trigger old memories that blur into other memories, a shifting reality Pat sorts through, trying to discover "What really happened."

Comic and sad, agonizing and illuminating, infuriating and hilarious, this ordinary day in the lives of ordinary people becomes a test of endurance, of reality, of love.

THE TEST

by Dorothy Bryant

FICTION

Ella Price's Journal
The Kin of Ata Are Waiting for You
Miss Giardino
The Garden of Eros
Prisoners
Killing Wonder
A Day in San Francisco
Confessions of Madame Psyche
The Test

NON-FICTION

Writing a Novel: Some Hints for Beginners

PLAYS

Dear Master
Tea With Mrs. Hardy

THE TEST

a novel by
Dorothy Bryant

Ata Books
Berkeley, California

Ata Books
1928 Stuart Street
Berkeley, California 94703
(510) 841-9613

Printed in the United States of America
Library of Congress Number: 91-072556
Cloth ISBN: 931688-15-9
Paper ISBN: 931688-16-7
First Edition

Cover: Robert Bryant
Editors: Betty Bacon, Kathy Vergeer,
        Lorri Ungaretti, Rose Weis

This one is for Rose

"Hello."

"Hi, Pat."

"Hello, Dad. How are you?"

"Oh . . . a little lonely."

"Yes. I know."

"You took a long time to answer the phone."

"I was in the shower."

"I thought you was coming down today."

"I am, Dad." I grope for my glasses, look at the clock. "It's only seven-thirty." I towel my wet hair while buttoning my shirt.

"When you coming?"

"I'll leave about nine, after the commute traffic clears. If nothing goes wrong on the freeway, I should be there by ten."

"But we'll be late for my test!"

"Your test isn't until four o'clock, Dad."

"Four?" Silence. Then, suspiciously, "You sure?"

"Look at the calendar, Dad." I wait for him to lift his eyes to the calendar above his wall phone.

"Uh . . . today is . . ."

"Friday, August twenty-first. See it? What does it say in that square? Friday, the twenty-first."

Another silence, longer this time. "D . . . M . . . V . . . four p.m."

"That's right, Dad. Department of Motor Vehicles, four p.m." I bought him a large daybook in which I write detailed plans, instructions, reminders, but he ignores it. He prefers his old way, the calendar sent yearly from the Italian Masonic Lodge, notes scrawled and squeezed into its tiny squares. This note has been there for a month, verified daily. I am almost glad the dread day has arrived. At least I will not have to repeat this ritual.

"Not until four? Flora said my test was at nine." She did not, but he would prefer that hour because he is anxious, and probably because he is fresher, more alert in the morning.

"No, Dad. Four o'clock."

"So when you coming down?"

"I'll be there by ten. We'll have plenty of time, if you want to go shopping, gas up the Chevy . . ."

"The truck's full up. We can use that."

"Remember, Dad, we agreed you would use the car this time."

"The pickup is easier, right out in the driveway. Why take the car out of the garage?"

"Remember, Dad, you failed one test because of mechanical problems." Was it the first? the third? I'm not sure how many attempts he has made. "Wasn't that one of the times you used the pickup?"

"That joker." His plaintive voice is suddenly gruff. "Give one of those guys a little power and . . . I tried to tell him all we had to do was stop in a gas station, put in a little brake fluid. I just lost brake fluid. He wouldn't listen. The only trouble was that . . ." That the truck won't start because it needs a new battery, won't stop because it needs new brakes, yet he somehow gets it moving and brings it to rest, several times a day. The master mechanic. "I was fixing cars, driving those dirt mountain roads before that guy was born, but he acted like . . ."

2

Like a very frightened man, I'll bet. Like my mother, who told Flora he could no longer maintain the truck or the car, that he didn't watch where he was driving. Flora told me, and I only shrugged. He hadn't watched for years. His wife watched and warned: street signs, turns, pedestrians, red lights and green, everything but speed limits, which he never even approached, always a dreamy driver, content to coast. My mother the navigator. When did the family joke wear thin, then turn into frightening reality?

". . . and then she hit me in the eye with that machine!"

He has drifted to the day he failed the vision test. Was that the day he failed the written test for the third time or the day he somehow passed it? The time before or after he made the "unsafe maneuver, FAILED" marked on one test paper but erased from his memory? I will never know what really happened during those ordeals because I refused to go along to witness them, tried to discourage his determined campaign to keep his driver's license. Today, the day of his final appeal, I have agreed to go with him, to be there when the verdict comes down on him.

"Dad, let's not talk now. If I'm going to leave here by nine, I have to get ready."

"Sure. Okay." He waits.

"See you about ten. Bye, Dad."

"Bye." He waits until I hang up.

My hand shakes as I pour my coffee. I had another bad night. The drowsy drift into sleep . . . then the sudden, familiar, icy wave of grief that so strangely resembles fear. Finally, sleep. Then the dream. My mother appeared. We embraced with pure joy. We talked. I told her all the things I never said, never knew I felt. She smiled beatifically. Then her smile faded. Her face broadened, lengthened, became the face of a man, my son, his eyes closed as he lay wasting, dying. No!

3

Shaken awake, my heart pounding, I checked the luminous hands of the clock. Five o'clock. I lay awake, calming myself by counting slow, even breaths, correcting the dream, point by point. My son is not dying. Joe is all right. It is his lover Mark who has AIDS. Joe is alive and well. For the present. And I cannot talk to my mother to tell her what I learned by losing her. She has been dead for more than a year— for fifteen months and two weeks, to be exact.

I turned over, shut my eyes, trying for another hour of sleep. In vain. So I put on my sweats and ran across the dim, nearly empty street to the park. An extra lap around the track is as good as an hour's sleep. Better. Was it Napoleon who said a good soldier needs to sweat every day? I needed a good sweat if I'm to get through this day's battle or, more precisely, massacre, escorting my father through his third loss in little more than a year. At eighty he lost his wife. Then he lost what little remained of his beloved garden. Now, after six months of fighting, he will lose his license to drive, while I— posing as his advocate—witness, welcome, enforce his defeat. This is my duty because Flora does more than her share, handling his bills and those endless forms for insurance and taxes.

The telephone rings.

"Hello."

"Hi, Pat."

"Yes, Dad."

"You coming down today?"

"Yes, Dad. We just talked a few minutes ago."

"Yeah, sure, I know."

Does he pretend, embarrassed, or being reminded, does he recall that he has just spoken to me? My mother complained—for how long, a year, two, three?—that , when they were alone, he would ask her the same question over and over

4

again. Questions? Innocuous enough, I thought, nothing to make her bite her lip with such fury. Now I have learned how a repeated, plaintive question can scratch a line into a groove into a raw wound, etched deeper and deeper. The ring of my telephone has become an alarm announcing another scrape through the wound.

"Was there something else, Dad?"

"Yeah, I want to know when you're coming down."

"I'll be there at ten."

"But my test is . . ."

"Leaving soon, Dad. I'm busy, have to get ready. Bye. See you soon. Bye." He waits. I hang up.

I take my coffee to the window and sit in the foggy light, traffic streaming below, humming and hooting, dammed, then rushing on again. Enough time to finish reading a story by a writer new to me, recommended by Joe. Called "What Really Happened," it is divided into eight parts, each describing the same experience of the same person in eight different voices. The voice of the first part is ten years old, of the second, twenty, then thirty, forty, decade by decade describing the same incident, each version uncovering a deeper truth until the eighty-year-old voice of the final part asks, with hopeless wisdom, "What Really Happened?"

The telephone rings.

Let it ring. Let him think I have already left. The ringing stops. I take a deep breath, but before I have fully exhaled, it begins again. I surrender.

"Hello."

"Hi." It is Flora. "Poor Pat. Got fed up, huh?"

"What?"

"Dad just called and told me."

"Told you what?"

"Didn't you tell him not to call you again? He said you

5

got really mad, told him to leave you alone, if you wanted to talk to him, you'd call him. He said he was afraid you weren't going to take him to his driving test and afraid to call you to find out. I calmed him down, told him you were bound to get mad if he kept pestering you."

"I didn't say anything like that. He called twice. I said I was coming, that's all. I certainly never told him not to call me, and I wasn't angry!" I certainly sound angry now. Defensive. Accused, therefore guilty of . . . something.

"Another confabulation." Flora takes comfort in using the new label we have learned.

"Or he confused me with someone else he called."

"Develia?" Flora pronounces the name as if she is grinding it between her teeth.

"Not likely. If she's so set on moving in, she wouldn't discourage his calls."

"Claudette?"

"Maybe. Or Hazel."

Two widows, old friends of my mother's, complain that he telephones them daily, insisting that they move in to keep house for him. (My father has used the telephone more in the past year than in the first eighty years of his life.) Maybe Claudette scolded him—last week, last month—her angry words sinking into his confused mind, then rising again, surfacing now with my name on them. Why me? Because today he is forced to depend on me, the bad daughter, the daughter he does not trust.

"I'll call him and reassure him I'm coming."

Flora sighs. "I'm really glad you're doing it, not me. Call me as soon as it's over."

We call each other daily, reporting new confabulations, checking them against reality, exchanging comfort across a hundred miles, discussing this now gigantic presence equidistant between us, our father. Our former differences blur like the three-year difference in our ages. We have begun to look more like sisters, less of my mother's long, angular face in mine, less of my father's round softness in Flora's, both of us fiftyish, graying, wrinkling.

"Anything new on Mark?" She never forgets to ask.

"Nothing good. The AZT isn't helping anymore. They're talking about a blood-cell transplant from his brother, to boost the immune cells."

"How's Joe doing?"

"Fine." I don't want to talk about him and Mark. Not today. Not both my father and my son today. "No news from Beth?" Flora's second daughter, three states away, reported false labor twice last week.

"Nothing. But the first two were late too."

"Call you later. Bye."

I hang up, take a deep breath, then punch the familiar numbers.

"Confabulation: a filling in of gaps in memory by free fabrication." That is all my old *Webster's* told me about this word my father's doctor dropped without explanation. "It's not only that he fills a memory gap," I tell my friends. "He fills it with a version he prefers to the truth, like insisting that he flunked his driver's test because his truck lost brake fluid. And, once formed, a confabulation is fixed, permanent. He forgets everything else, but never his own invention. He records it on some tape in his head, then plays it over and over, word for word, exactly the same."

"Like our dear president," my younger friends laugh. They like taking political views, global views. They also hope to dilute my intensity. They feel uncomfortable hearing my furious complaints about a failing old man, just as I felt about my mother's complaints. An older friend listens in silent

7

sympathy. Her father, a courtly, charming, ninety-year-old retired professor of philosophy, who lives in her house, has lately begun to accuse her of poisoning his food.

"Hello?"

"Hi, Dad. Just wanted to tell you I'm leaving now."

"I'm sorry I bothered you." His plaintive uncertainty has turned into a whine. "If you don't want me to call . . . I only wanted to make sure you . . ."

"You didn't bother me, Dad."

"I didn't mean to make you mad."

"I'm not mad."

"But if I can never even call you . . . in case I need . . ."

"I didn't tell you not to call me."

". . . something. I'm so alone here, but if you want me to wait till you call me . . . don't get mad, but suppose I need to ask you . . ."

"Dad, I didn't tell you not to call me. Maybe it was someone else. Not me!" My voice is rising. I swallow, breathe deeply.

"But you said if you wanted to talk to me, you'd . . ."

"I didn't say anything like that." I keep my voice soft, calm. "I'm glad when you call because then I know you're all right. If I didn't hear from you, I'd be afraid something happened."

That he had fallen from the apple tree again, or had coasted, brakeless, into another car or over an unlucky pedestrian, or had broken down in the middle of an intersection and was sitting there lost and terrified, traffic coming at him. Or his angina pains had turned into a real attack, and he lay helpless on the kitchen floor, unable to call us for help, unable to answer our calls. It's true. The only thing worse than the constant ringing of my phone is silence.

"But if I can never call you . . ."

8

"You can, Dad. Call me any time."

"It's the loneliness. If I just had someone here . . . she could do a little cooking, cleaning. There's this woman . . ."

This woman. That woman. He never says her name. Develia.

"Look, Dad, we can talk about that later. We'll have all day. I have to . . ."

"What? Who's that? Someone at the back door?"

"Probably Rosetta, Dad."

"Rosetta? What does she want?"

"It's Friday, Dad, remember? She always comes to clean on Friday."

"I don't need . . ."

I hear Rosetta's voice. "*Ciao*, Pete."

I grab my chance to hang up. "I'm leaving now, Dad. See you in about an hour. Bye."

I drive toward the Wharf, park illegally (how else?) at Giulio's, order a "Captain's Plate to go," then go outside to a fruit stall, where I buy a single pear. I sit down to wait on a bench over the water, watchful for traffic patrol. The fog is brightening, a hard white light, a hope of sun breaking through. The Captain's Platter, bits of fish, breaded and fried, has been okayed by Doctor Rayman despite salt, cholesterol, and God knows what else, because for the first time in his life my father is too thin. I have learned what will prod his feeble appetite now that he has become such a fussy eater.

Become? It dawns on me that he has always been a fussy eater. During those childhood years when Flora and I were required—for reasons merging economics, health, and morality—to eat anything and everything put on our plates, I

9

hardly realized that what was put on our plates was what my father liked.

A scene surfaces from deep memory. As a still-teenaged bride, I invited my parents to dinner to show off my skill at learning my mother's polenta and chicken. I added a touch of my own, a slight variation in the dressing I put on the salad. As always with food he liked, my father ate the polenta and chicken without comment. When the salad was served, he lifted a leaf of lettuce to his mouth, stopped, sniffed it, looked at it, slowly placed it on his tongue. As he chewed and swallowed, he raised his eyebrows and shrugged—gestures that indicated there was nothing essentially wrong with the foreign taste. Then he put down his fork and left the rest of the salad on his plate, an act that created a terrible silence, like a fog of failure spreading over the table. Tony—also an over-fed Italian son—behaved the same way when he was served anything but steak and pasta. During our dozen years together, he lost weight.

My father's tastes have changed drastically since I was a child, but are still non-negotiable. The carefully balanced stew Flora leaves for him will rot in the refrigerator while he makes do with a can of soup. But this crusted, greasy, over-seasoned fish he will eat with birdlike gusto, picking away at it, spreading it over two meals, maybe three. Will he stretch it too far and poison himself, torn between the equal pleasures of tasting and hoarding? Not if I sit with him, eat a bit, talk, distract him so that he will forget, will eat half a portion instead of saving most of it.

I am on the freeway exactly at nine, with the traffic thinning and the sun definitely breaking through. It will be hot in Sequoia Park. I locate myself on the center lane. I have learned that I can stay there, rolling past interchanges and turnoffs all the way to the Sequoia turnoff. No changing lanes or checking signs to clutter my mind. With ordinary caution, I am free to daydream, even to confabulate arriving to find my father miraculously, reasonably, giving up his determination to drive. A vain wish, a conscious fantasy, therefore not a true confabulation.

Doctor Rayman dropped that word from on high when, shortly after the funeral, I took my mother's place, accompanying my father to the monthly checkup, reporting some astonishing invention of my father's that had taken several phone calls to straighten out. Rayman, my parents' doctor for thirty years, releases information sparingly, issues unexplained directives, decorates his obvious limitations with stiff, dignified indifference, keeping his eyes averted to avoid presumptuous familiarity, to discourage my insistent questions. His favorite trick is letting my question hang in silence, turning away as if it were stupid or offensive. If I wait long enough, he will eventually turn back and, still without looking at me, utter a monosyllabic evasion. Doctor Rayman was civil to me only once, even kind, when my mother was hospitalized again just after my father's eightieth birthday celebration. That was how I knew that this time she would die.

I turn on my old car radio to the only classical music station it receives. Predictably, an aria from *Traviata* is ending. It is followed by one from *Bohème*.

During the week of my mother's dying, Flora and I took turns staying all night with my father. During the day I sat beside my mother's hospital bed, watching her unconscious body breathe. In the evening I sat beside my father, listening to his mechanically repeated phrases, automatic as breathing, waiting for him to go to bed—early, thank God—so I could sit alone, the television holding off silence and thought. There were two Italian operas on television during that week. I thought I knew every note of those old chestnuts. Now I seemed to understand them for the first time, to realize that Italian opera is about death.

My friends say that because my mother was dying, I now associate Verdi and Puccini with death. Yes, of course, elementary, psychologically correct, indisputable, and irrelevant. What I suddenly realize goes beyond personal association. At last I see why my old Austrian professor of music theory despised this music on theological grounds. It vibrates solely within the range of human life, each note (even the light songs, especially the light songs) an abject, unashamed cry against the decay of human flesh. It offers no reconciliation like a requiem by Brahms or Fauré, no transcendence of grief, no hope, no God. If, beyond the easy, sentimental stereotypes, there is, after all, any trait that is Italian, it must be this yielding to a pure agony of grief for the end of each human life.

It is unlike me to give way to this romantic music. I am, after all, a daughter of the Piedmontese, northern Italians, reserved, prudent, orderly. Our sadness is not operatic, but chill and gray, like the fog of the Turinese plain at the foot of the French Alps.

I turn the radio dial to the jazz station and get a wild new set of variations on "How High the Moon." Better.

My friends suggest a grief support group. I nod and change the subject. Simone Weil knew. "The absence of the dead is their way of appearing to us." I do not want to join a group where I can talk away the pain and regret that haunt me. They are my mother's way of appearing to me. Her sad ghost gleams in the sunlight on the tiny amber vase she gave me. It traces its outline through a mile of her embroidery around a tablecloth too fine and formal for my table (and how she hated that pattern by the time she finished it). Her ghost speaks in her disciplined, symmetrical script passing on a family recipe I never took the trouble to make. It is woven into the crocheted afghan I gather around myself when I lie, sleepless, on the couch, remembering that she made it during those endless hours in front of the television with my father repeating his questions over and over. I am surrounded, haunted by her presence in gifts I had once assigned a place, and then forgot, as I had managed to assign her a small place outside my "real" life, lest she meddle, scold, grieve, sicken at my, to her, strange and perilous life.

Talking away this haunting pain would resemble the maudlin discharge of emotion my mother hated, the hypocrisy of retroactive love: her widowed mother, recalling her *caro marito* who, during his last year, drew a line through the middle of their tiny cottage, dividing their mutual hatred into separate wastelands; her uncle, who spat on his wife during their almost daily quarrels, then wept conspicuously for his lost *buon' anima* at her grave. My mother viewed these extravagant mourners with contempt. "If you really love someone, you show it while they're alive."

My daughter insists that I did show love for my mother when she was alive. No, Amy. I gave my mother certain minimal, proper, and safe signs of a show of love, and, near the end, when I might have lowered my defenses, might have spoken, closed the distance I maintained—but all this, Amy sensibly asserts, is not What Really Happened. It is grief disguised as guilt, a useless weight to be shrugged off. My son agrees. His mixed feelings toward me he refers to as "the mother-son-thing," as natural as the law of gravity, taken for granted. "When you die," he says, "I'll feel sad but not guilty." I thought, but did not say, "Believe me, Joe, you don't know how you'll feel." Lately we do not speculate on my death, it being unlikely that he will live to see it.

Suddenly I am at the Sequoia Park turnoff, well before ten o'clock. Another mile, two turns, and I will be at my father's house. I had almost begun to enjoy the drive, pretending (confabulating?) that I could drive on forever, never arriving.

Off Redwood Road, I turn down quiet, empty streets of low houses behind lawns and occasional old fruit trees left from the days when only orchards stood here. I turn into the broad driveway and pull up beside the old pickup. The sliding garage door is open, and my father is stooped over something on the ground between the door and the pickup. As I get out of my car, I hear him cursing softly. He hears me, straightens up and turns, a small figure in a pale blue shirt and loose tan cotton pants, his face red with anger under the little straw hat that protects him from the sun.

"What is it, Dad? What's wrong?"

"That dirty crook, he took me."

"Who? What's that?" We stand together over an old cardboard box on the concrete. It contains a rusted square of scrap metal that was once a car battery.

"That guy down at Andy's, you know, on the corner of Redwood and Fourth."

"The garage," I nod.

"I took the pickup down there for him to put the battery on the charger. But he kept saying I needed a new battery, so I let him sell me this one, and it doesn't work."

"That's not a new battery, Dad."

14

"I know that! Reconditioned, twenty percent off."

"That's not even reconditioned, Dad, it's a mess."

"That's what I'm telling you!" His voice breaks as his anger becomes impotent frustration. "It won't work. I can't even . . ."

"He sold you that? You paid him money?"

"I got the receipt right here."

He hands me a sheet of crumpled yellow paper. I can make nothing of it but the address of Andy's Garage. I open the trunk of my car.

"What are you doing?"

"I'm going to take this back and get your money back. Look, Dad, just go into the house and take it easy. Get out of this hot sun. Go on in. I'll take care of it. Don't worry. I'll be back in five minutes. You go in and rest."

He watches as I bend over the box. My first attempt to lift it fails. He moves toward me. "No, Dad, I'll do it. You shouldn't even try." I bend my knees in proper lifting mode, grip the box, and hoist the rusty mess into the trunk of my car.

During the half-mile drive to Andy's Garage, I rehearse what I will say to the kind of person who would take advantage of a confused old man. I turn into the wide lot, stopping directly in front of the door of the tiny office, get out, yank open the trunk and leave it gaping as I put my head into the empty office and shout, "Anybody here?"

A man my age comes around the side of the building, wiping his grease-blackened hands on a rag nearly as black. "Help you?"

"Did you sell this to Mr. Sancavei?"

"No," he says, without looking into my trunk.

"He wasn't in here today?"

"Yeah, he just left. I told him . . . hey! Aren't you his daughter? Pat? You don't remember me. I'm George Leary. We were in the same class at Redwood High."

I peer at the pale, jowly face and the white hair, then remember that it once was flaming red. "George. Of course, I remember you." Quiet, smiling George, who patiently endured high school, as unhappy as I, but for different reasons. "I remember now. Andy is your uncle. You used to work here after school."

"Right. Then I went in the army, tried some other stuff, but came back. I bought the place about fifteen years ago."

I nod. "You always loved working on cars. I remember how you used to come into my folks' store . . ." That is, I am beginning to remember, bits and pieces of a freckled teenager coming together.

"Yeah, your mom was something. Her and that catalog, thick as four phone books. But she could always find whatever you needed. Lina the Brain of Sancavei Auto Parts, that's what we all called her."

"You know she died last year."

"Yeah, I'm sorry. Your dad is lost without her. He really shouldn't be all alone there."

"I know."

"How's Tony? You married Tony Maretti, right?

"We broke up."

"Oh, sorry."

I shake my head and smile. "Twenty years ago. I moved to the city and sort of lost touch. You and . . . uh . . . Sally Larson got married, right?"

"Right. Thirty-two years now. Four grandchildren. You got any grandchildren?"

I shake my head.

"You still singing? I remember you sang the solo in . . . what was that opera?"

"Gilbert and Sullivan. *Yeoman of the Guard.*"

"That was it. I tell my kids, but they can't believe we did stuff like that in high school! I always thought you'd turn pro if you didn't get married and have a family and all. You were great."

I laugh and shake my head. "Good, not great. I studied music when I went back to college, but that's no way to make a living."

"Gave it up," he concludes, sadly.

"No, I still sing in the symphony chorus. Oh, and sometimes I sing songs with my ESL students."

"ESL?"

"English as a second language. Teaching foreigners, immigrants mostly. I teach Cambodians and Salvadorans to sing 'Home on the Range' and 'We Shall Overcome.'"

He laughs. "Sounds like steady work. You like it?"

"I love it."

"So, what can I do for you?"

"Well . . . my father told me he bought this here." I hand him the yellow slip and point into the trunk of my car.

He whistles and shakes his head. "Wonder where he got that. Must have been laying around his garage for twenty years." Then he looks at the yellow slip and frowns. "This could be the receipt for the battery I sold him ten years ago. Yeah, look, you can just barely see the date." He shakes his head. "He still had that receipt!"

"My mother kept very careful records." But how did he ever dig it out?

"He keeps coming in and asking me to put it on the charger. So I do it, but I keep telling him he needs a new battery. This morning I said I'd give him twenty percent off

17

for old time's sake. He said he'd think about it. Did he tell you I sold him that mess?"

I feel a flush of shame rising as I look into his honest, patient face. "He . . . gets confused."

"You're telling me. Whenever I see that old truck of his coming down the street, wandering along, cars honking, passing him right and left, and no signal or anything when he turns in . . . you know, Pat, I don't want to stick my nose in, but he shouldn't drive anymore. You ought to talk to him."

I can only nod and try to get away from here. "How much is a new battery?" I pull out my checkbook and follow him into the office, where he insists on giving me the twenty percent discount. The truck will be easier to sell with a new battery in it. Or easier to drive away and hide, if he insists on driving it without a license. Flora and I can't decide just what we will do next.

As George puts the new battery into my trunk, he says, "You want me to take this piece of junk and get rid of it?"

"I'd appreciate it."

"Sure, no problem." Then he laughs. "But what'll I do if tomorrow your father shows up and wants it back?"

"I don't think he'll be driving after today."

"Good."

"I'm sorry about the mix-up."

He shrugs. "Hey . . . we all get old, right?"

All the way back, I repeat George's sensible words, alternately calmed and frightened by them. Dying, I have accepted. Growing old is something else.

When I turn into my father's driveway again, the garage door is closed, my father nowhere in sight. I get out and open the cab of the truck. Then I open my trunk and grab the new battery by the strap-handle. One good hoist, turn, swing, and I have deposited it on the floor of the truck cab. I set the lock and close the door. My car blocks the garage door; later we will have to get the Chevy out. So I back out and park on the street behind Rosetta's car.

I walk up the driveway, past the front garden. The grass is browner than last week, the roses drooping, petals dry and blown, scattered on the grass. I pull the hose out from the side of the house, attach the sprinkler and turn on a light spray, just high enough to wet the patch of grass up to the edge of the roses. Maybe he won't hear the water running, at least not until some of it wets the struggling plants.

Only the bougainvillea over the front porch looks healthy, probably because its roots dig in beside the water pipe (another leak? remember to check). Thickly clustered blossoms gleam like fresh blood spilled over the roof, running along the rain gutters. The vines clog the gutters, clutch the roof shingles. Stains streak the stucco wall and garage door, tracks of unchanneled rain streaming in all directions. Something must be done before fall rains start, but Flora says he panics when she takes out pruning shears, as if she is robbing him.

I walk past the front porch to the left side of the house. I am of a family that does not use front doors, like farm people, like servants. The narrow gate is stuck open, held in the twisted branches of an overgrown rosemary bush. I push through and walk along the narrow path beside the low fence. The neighbor's Doberman barks wildly as I walk the length of the house, and I smile gratefully at him. This house sits so unprotected. The locks he still remembers to fasten before bedtime are no obstacle for modern burglars. An old man alone. Even in the suburbs, terrible things happen.

I tap a signal on the kitchen window as I pass it and sing out "Hello!" then round the corner of the house to open the back door. I enter, pass the water heater and washing machine, then stop in the open doorway to the kitchen. "I'm back."

He is rising from the recliner chair in the television alcove in the far corner. He crosses the room toward me, moving with nimble, short, quick steps that remind me of the fast one-step he danced at Italian picnics fifty years ago. Age shortens our steps to the "baby steps" of the old childhood game. ("Mother, may I take one giant step?" No, you may take three baby steps.) At least my father's steps are quick and agile, not the slow, painful inching along of my mother's final steps.

We meet half-way across the room near the table. I put my arms around him, reaching down slightly to his shoulders. I grew to his height in my teens, and now he has shrunken. His blue chambray shirt and tan pants hang loosely. Underneath he wears long underwear, even now in summer. The perspiration smell is strong today. Last week I got him to shower when I arrived, by threatening to leave unless he did. Evidently no one else has been so cruel since then.

I kiss his cheek. Stubble scrapes my face as my eyes measure the fringe of hair skirting the back of his bald head: nearly two inches. Flora forgot to mention that she had no luck trying to get him to the barber. He stiffens, arms hanging limp, and accepts my kiss—not a physically affectionate man.

I hardly ever saw him kiss my mother. I don't remember sitting on his lap or being hugged when I was small. By the same token, there are no secret horrors of incest in our family, like those filling newspapers and books today. I wonder if his generation of men was not cold, after all, only careful to freeze unmentionable possibilities. I know—from a suddenly

20

confiding comment of my mother just before she died—that sex is very important to my father, that he felt bitterly humiliated at his loss of potency, that Doctor Rayman deemed it "good for him to try," in effect prescribing that this weary, ill woman encourage this impotent old child to go through the motions upon her. She also confided that it was during one such attempt that she had one of her heart "incidents," caused surely, not by passion, but by resentful, suppressed rage. Why did she put up with it? Why did she tell me, not Flora?

"What time is it?"

"Ten-fifteen."

"You said you'd be here by ten."

"I was. Before ten. Remember, I went to straighten out that business about the battery."

"Oh, yeah." He seems to have lost interest.

"I got you a new battery, put it in the cab of the truck. When Teddy comes by, he can install it for you."

"I don't need a new battery! The one I have is . . ."

"Didn't cost you anything, Dad. All paid for. I just exchanged the other one for it."

This absurd lie satisfies him. He shrugs and loses interest again.

"It's awfully hot in here, Dad. You don't have the furnace on, do you?"

"No, no. I always just turn it on a little when I get up in the morning, and then . . ."

Probably when Rosetta arrived, she turned it off. I move to the sink and open the window above it.

"No, no, it makes a draft!"

"There's no draft on a day like this. There's no air at all in here!" In one of my panic scenarios when he is slow to answer the phone, I see him sitting in his recliner, facing a blaring television, dead, stifled. "Let me open it, just a little?"

"Just a little," he concedes, sliding the window two inches from the frame. Windows closed, furnace on, long underwear, reluctance to bathe—attempts to keep away a chill that settles in aged, sluggish blood? Yet his skin is pink and healthy (except for the telltale red lines spreading from his nose), and less wrinkled than mine. His blue eyes need glasses only for reading. His teeth are sound, his hearing excellent.

"We going for my test now?"

"No, Dad, not until four."

"What time is it now?" He is facing the refrigerator, which stands under a large wall clock. But he looks at me, not at the clock.

"Ten-twenty. I had a nice drive down. Traffic wasn't bad. You know, they're talking about putting in trains again. That would be great, if I could just hop onto a high-speed train, read a book, and . . ."

"What time is my test!"

"Four."

He is not interested in news of projects or incidents outside of what he knows, what he lives. Certainly not in any idea of riding in a train instead of in one's own private automobile.

"I brought you a Captain's Plate." I pull the tray out of its paper bag. He looks at it blankly, the annoyance only slowly leaving his face. "You know, Dad, that seafood you like. We can just warm it up tonight." I am rewarded by a flicker of anticipatory pleasure in his eyes. Suddenly they narrow with alarm.

"What's that noise? Rosetta got the water on outside? What the hell does she . . ."

"No, no, it was me." I mustn't give him any excuse to

22

harass Rosetta. "I turned on the water out in front."

"Why'd you do that!" he demands, alarmed, outraged.

"Dad, everything's dying out there. You have to water those roses or . . ."

"I water them, I water them, but not in full sun. Don't you know . . . the time to water is sundown."

"If you remember." But by sundown he is too muddled and lethargic. Or does he simply hope to reduce his water bill?

"I'll remember."

"When was the last time you watered out in front?"

Hesitation. "Last night."

"Oh, come on, Dad, that grass is bone dry, the ground cracking like . . ."

"I'll water it tonight!" He glares at me, angry and astonished at my interference. I stand my ground, refuse his silent demand that I go out to turn off the water. At least the flowers will have another two minutes of water before he can get out there to turn it off. Besides, the exercise will be good for him. I open the refrigerator, ducking under his angry glare as I concentrate on putting the Captain's Plate inside. I put my single golden pear in the empty fruit bowl on top of the refrigerator.

He quick-steps toward the back door, plucking his little green straw hat from above the washing machine, putting it on before he opens the door.

It is automatic, this reaching for his hat, covering his bald head before stepping outside even for a few moments, winter or summer, light or dark. According to an old family story, I once asked my father why he had no hair, and he answered, "Your mother got mad at me and pulled it all out." Pleased with his joke, he repeated it often. I remember the repetitions, the chuckles and smiles, but not my asking him. I must have been very young. I knew it was a joke, but as a child I always half-believed my mother angry enough to pull his hair, though there was never a quarrel, never a voice raised.

All the old snapshots, taken outdoors, show his face in shadow under a hat. Only one formal photo, with his sister Eva, taken when he was sixteen, shows him with thick, curly blond hair. Shortly after that picture was taken—according to another old family story—a boy gave my father a bottle of "hair straightener" to help him conform to the current fashion. His hair came out in handfuls while his mother sobbed and his father cursed. It never grew back. A practical joke. Were people more cruel in those days? The cruelty of the half-century of my life has surpassed any in history, yet it seems less personal, less mean and vindictive than casually giving a naive boy the means to disfigure himself.

Yet is this story really closer to the truth than the joke about my mother? In the dialect spoken by my grandparents, our family name means "hairless." Did the cruel practical joke only hasten a process so genetically inevitable that it became the identification of my father's family? What Really Happened?

The back door opens and closes again, and he is beside me between the refrigerator and the sink. "We going for my test?"

"Not until four, Dad."

"What time is it now?"

"A little after ten. We have the whole day if you want to do some shopping, go to the barber?" I drop a hint he shows no sign of hearing. We stand in silence while I try to think of something to say that will interest him. "Is your back okay now? No more pain?" Since he fell from the apple tree— actually from the rotted-out, home-made ladder that literally shattered under his meager weight—we have this adventure to review each week.

"Not bad now. I was sure lucky Teddy was just getting here. He heard me calling." His voice picks up in interest, resonance. "I was on the ground, kind of in shock. I didn't know if I was hurt bad. He took me to the hospital, but the X rays were fine, bones of a man half my age, the doctor said. I was sure lucky Teddy happened to come by." The tone of his voice begins to sag. "What would have happened if . . ." He shakes his head. "I shouldn't be alone here. It's the loneliness that kills you. Alone here all the time. Nobody."

"Dad, you're not alone all the time. I come every Wednesday, Flora on Mondays. Rosetta cleans on Fridays, and Aunt Eva drops by on Saturday. Then with one of the grandchildren usually showing up on a Sunday, and Eva's grandchildren once in a while, there's someone coming by almost every day."

"So what? Something could happen right after they leave! And what if I got sick or something during the night?"

"That's true. That's why Flora wanted you to look at a couple of retirement communities where you'd have . . ."

"You're not putting me in one of those places!"

"Not a nursing home, Dad. If you'd just go and look at a couple of them. One's in Santa Rina, right near Flora. You'd have your own apartment. Meals are served, and there'd be other people around, things to do, even trips to Reno. You haven't been able to go up and play the slots for a long time. Or you could come up to the city and take an apartment in my building." I'd have to evict someone. And what about later, when Joe might need to be nearby? Relax. An apartment in the city, near me, is the last thing he would consider. Why am I repeating this old script? We have given up trying to get him out of this house, a mistake that makes him distrust our every suggestion. The sight and touch of the familiar is his only comfort, his only security.

"When I leave here, it'll be in a pine box! I have a lovely home right here, everything I ever wanted. Except . . . all I need is someone to stay here . . . do a little cooking . . . a little cleaning. She wouldn't even have to pay me rent. It's a good deal for some woman on a pension. Someone who . . ." He hesitates, then carefully pronounces, "There's . . . this woman . . ."

Develia. I know this is the time for me to tell him we have caved in, ended the year-long battle, surrendered. I have chosen the words, rehearsed them: It's your decision, Dad. Why don't I say them? Later. "This Woman" will come up again, inevitably. I'll say my new lines next time. "I haven't said hello to Rosetta yet. Is she cleaning the front room? I'll just go in and say hello."

I go through the doorway beside the refrigerator, into the L-shaped dining and living room, dim, stale spaces entered for cleaning by Rosetta every week, but otherwise closed off, used only for infrequent guests or family gatherings, the most recent being after my mother's funeral. When my parents built this house twenty-five years ago, they bought new rugs, chairs, tables, couch, dining set—cheap department store "modern," with none of the character of their discarded mohair couch and oak table. (Or, recreating them in my imagination, am I adding character?) For twenty-five years these drapes, rugs, chairs, tables, were cleaned and polished as they faded into unused shabbiness. The walls are nearly bare, dominated by a huge, hideous acrylic painting above the fireplace, an "oriental" river valley in bilious greens, another "bargain" my father boasted of buying from the stock of men who used to stand near freeway approaches selling blankets and rugs and velvet paintings. (An ink drawing of my daughter by a good local artist, a gift from me, hangs in shadow behind the unused front door.)

26

I hate that garish painting. I hate my own snobbery.

Rosetta is not here. She has finished these rooms, leaving the drapes on the window to the front garden slightly open. A slit of light shines on the round table under the window, gleaming on the gold-framed photo of my mother and father taken at their golden wedding anniversary party. An inscription carved on the frame reads,

Lina and Pete

"Grow old along with me

The best is yet to be"

During the five years after that party my mother occasionally recited those lines bitterly as her weakness and pain increased. "Well," I said, "Browning was probably only forty when he wrote that." Did I actually say that to her, or did I only think it? Is it a wry joke we shared or one I only wish we had shared? What Really Happened?

I leave the living room, walking down a hall past two closed, unused bedrooms. At the end of the hall I find Rosetta in my parents' bedroom, leaning over my mother's vanity table, dusting a framed photo of Flora and me, aged thirteen and ten, in twin plaid dresses with white lace collars crocheted by our grandmother.

"Eh, Patrizia, *come va?*"

"*Bene, e tu?*" I cock my head in the general direction of the kitchen and my father. "*Tutto* okay?"

"*Si, si.* Sure. Okay." Rosetta shrugs, keeps on with her work. She is about my age, taller and thinner, the final and most recent immigrant of our family, having arrived twenty-five years ago. She speaks broken English with a sprinkling of Italian, like my broken Italian mixed with English. Somehow we manage to communicate.

"New water heater okay?"

"Sure. Much better."

"Thanks for letting us know. I don't know what we'd do without you." She only shrugs again, knowing I am right.

She began cleaning for my mother eight years ago, when the final downward slide of illness began. Every Friday she came, worked, ate lunch with my mother. When my mother died, the depth of Rosetta's grief took me by surprise. I still hear echoes of the anguish in her whispered "Lina, oh, Li-na" as she knelt by the coffin. Every week for years she had been here, helping, talking, seeing, knowing. She knew my mother's final years as I had not—admit it—as I had chosen not to know them. I feel a slight twinge of jealousy. She was more a daughter to my mother than I was, though not the daughter my mother wanted, any more than I was. Wrong. Not What Really Happened. My mother simply wanted me to be happy and successful in a way she could understand. Still not right. Even Flora didn't completely satisfy . . . that's it. Nothing we did or became could satisfy my mother's own deprivation. No one ever lived through her children, least of all one who thought she should.

"Flora talked to you about the new arrangement?"

"Huh? Oh, sure, sure."

"I'll send you the check." I want to make sure she understands. "She told you we'd pay more? Is it enough? Is it what you get in your other places?"

"*Si, si.*" She averts her eyes, uncomfortable with this discussion of money among family.

"So, no matter what he says, you keep coming every Friday."

"Okay." It is her memorial to my mother that she continues to clean the house though she now refuses to eat here. Not that, lonely as he is, my father would invite her. I'm sure that when he looks at her he sees only the money she has cost him.

We ask about each other's families, and both of us skip the bad parts. I keep Joe's ordeal, Mark's illness, to myself, and she says, "Donardi *sta bene.*" My mother once said you could tell when a wife really disliked her husband. "She calls him by his last name." Rosetta's marriage, to an older Italian immigrant, is in the tradition of my grandparents: conflict and bitterness, till death do them part.

My father is seated in front of his paper place mat and dishes, already set for lunch on the gray formica kitchen table. I sit down opposite him. "Well, Rosetta is a gem, Dad. We're so lucky that she . . ."

"I don't need her. What do I dirty, here all alone?"

"There are a lot of little things that keep a house neat, especially as clean as you're used to."

"I can do it. I do my own cooking, wash dishes, like I always helped your mother after she started getting sick."

"There are more things than washing dishes to . . ."

"All I need is to learn how to run the washing machine." He half rises. "You could show me right now."

"The directions are on the lid, Dad." I stay in my chair, refusing to take him through that process again, only to watch him lose his way among the simple dials. Besides, the struggle has escalated to making him change his clothes so they can be washed.

He sits down again and shifts to another part of this script. "I don't need her every week. She could come once a month or so."

I take my cue, repeat my lines. "She would have to take another job. She wouldn't have a day free to come irregularly."

"I don't need her. I told her not to come next week. I let her go. She's not coming anymore. She has too many other jobs."

29

"Listen, Dad!" I lean forward. "Listen to me."

His mouth trembles. "I'm sorry, don't get mad at me."

"I'm not mad at you, Dad." Will he really relent, give up his efforts to get rid of Rosetta, efforts which—I hate realizing this—must have begun long before my mother died?

"I didn't mean to bother you. I guess I phoned you too many times. It's just that I'm so lonely, and sometimes I get scared. If I can't even call you . . ."

"You can call me anytime you want to."

"But you said . . ."

"I didn't, Dad. Whatever it was, I didn't say it. Maybe it was Claudette. You phone her too often, and she has to rest because of her heart. Maybe you called when she was sleeping, and she didn't want to be disturbed." His expression is almost blank, the way I look at him when I know he is confabulating. "Call me anytime, Dad, anytime." I can't tell if I have made him believe me. I can't even remember what we were talking about. Oh, yes. "Now, about Rosetta. I'm going to . . ."

"I don't need her," he growls.

"I think you do. I told her to keep coming every Friday, and—no, just listen, Dad—I'm going to pay her. For my own peace of mind. It's worth it to me. I don't want you to let her go and then find that you need her more than ever and we can't get her back. Then I'd have to go through hell to find someone. You know how hard it is to find the right person, to make sure I've brought someone into your house we can trust. I can't be here all the time to make sure. Rosetta is family, she's good, she knows this house and just what to do." I do not repeat Flora's and my vow that we'll be damned before we'll come here as free maids. "You understand? She's going to keep coming, and I'll pay. It won't cost you a dime. I'll take care of it, just like the battery, just like the water heater."

He stares at me for a moment, then averts his eyes, sits very still, then shrugs his acceptance. We can throw away that part of the script, never again argue the need for Rosetta, never again call to beg her to return after he has fired her.

I should feel only relief, but my stronger feeling is shame. I am ashamed of the suppressed smile quivering on his lips, ashamed of the devious satisfaction settling on his face, loosening his jaw, as he savors his triumph. After months of dogged struggle he has rid himself, not of Rosetta, but of the slow, painful ritual of reaching into his wallet and extracting a twenty dollar bill. He has won the game, has tricked his daughter into paying.

No, he has been out-tricked, outfoxed. "For his own good," Flora says firmly. "The doctor said so. Amy, too. Why call it a trick? He signed the papers." Never mind whether or not he knew what he was signing. It was all quite legal, and now we can dip into his funds to pay for Rosetta, for the water heater, for the battery, for all his needs. It's simpler to pretend that we are paying. We have learned the secret of ending certain battles. Let him believe he is making us pay while he hoards more money. Comforting to him and easy for us. Then why do I feel so ashamed?

"What time is my test?"

"Four."

"What time is it now?"

"Ten-thirty-five."

"Is that all?" Now he looks at the clock; does he think I'm lying? Or that I can't tell time? "Not even time for lunch yet."

He turns and looks toward the alcove where the television stands faced by two brown vinyl recliner chairs. Against the wall behind one of the recliners stands a small desk, its hinged writing flap closed up. My parents gave the desk to Flora on her fifteenth birthday, but the only space for it in our old house was against a wall in the dining room, forbidden

31

territory except during holiday family meals. Gradually it was filled up with the bills and ledgers of my father's shop. Now, since our mother's death, this desk finally is Flora's province.

He turns his glance regretfully away from the desk. If I were Flora, he would quick-step over to the desk, pull down the flap, take out his three bank books, and bring them to the table. Then he would ask Flora to write down on a slip of paper the balance in each of the accounts, add them up, read the total to him, discuss the minor variations as interest is added or taxes subtracted. This ritual takes up the first hour of Flora's weekly visit. Afterward, Flora puts the list of figures, the total circled, into one of the bank books. When she returns the next week, the list has disappeared, and she must make a new one. She believes he destroys the list so as to have the pleasure of watching her write down, add up, and then recite to him again the figure of his worth. His worth. I mean no irony or disrespect. This is his own, proud measure of himself.

There was a time long ago when I was allowed to help my father count his money. In fact, I have almost no other memory of my father from my childhood, when he spent every day at the shop, returning home after I was in bed. Once a week—was it on Sundays, when he opened up later?—I ate my breakfast cereal at one corner of the kitchen table while he emptied a long canvas sack and counted the change he would put into the cash register. Coins rolled, jingled, spread across the table, a vast treasure to a child in those days when a penny taken to a local store would buy a colorful package containing candy and a "prize," chosen from dozens of dazzling and mysterious packages.

I rarely had a penny. There was The Depression, no pennies to spare. "You are lucky to have a house and warm clothes, good food and a doctor whenever you get sick."

"Daddy's got lots of money in the sack," I answered, creating a family joke that surpassed my father's joke about his baldness. The joke became the emblem of my perceived impracticality, my vague, bookish dreaminess. I was always mistrusted, not for lack of honesty or intelligence, but for lack of "common sense."

Yet I did actually steal from my father one morning when I knelt on my chair, elbows on the table, "helping" by making stacks of pennies, nickels, dimes. Slowly, carefully, keeping one eye on my father, I put my elbow on a penny, then slid it closer and closer to the edge of the table until it fell into my lap. I slid it into the pocket of my dress, where it stayed for the rest of the day, growing to an unbearable weight, heating to fiery temperature, too heavy and hot to carry to the candy store. By dinner time I was unable to eat. My mother felt my forehead—was I going to be sick again?

That night I lay awake in bed, waiting for the sounds of my father's return, waiting for my mother to go to bed and leave him sitting at the kitchen table listening to the radio. Then I got up, went to him, put the penny on the table. "You dropped it," I recited my carefully rehearsed words. "I found it on the floor."

Was that when I drew a sharp line between me and my father's money? (Yes, even my mother, who earned most of it and managed all of it, called it his money, his shop.) I never felt entitled to anything, felt always like a beggar, a burden, a drain on the limited earnings of my overworked parents.

Now that we have learned there is more money than we thought, my hands-off unease about it has only increased. I want him to use it up before he dies, trade it for comforts he rejects—nothing comforts him like counting his money. (Depression hangover? A friend's aged mother cites Depression memories as she compulsively buys and buys with every penny of her pension.) I back off from it, push it out of my mind, almost to the point of negligence. If it were up to me, his money and all chance for the comforts it could buy him, might already be lost to the infamous Develia or some other predator, so reluctant have I been to take a grip on it. Fortunately for my father, Flora scented the danger, gave the alarm, persuaded him to sign, tricked him into safeguarding his worth.

"One thing I got to do is to sell that lot."

The lot again. I say nothing, but he goes on as if I have taken my cue and asked him why.

"I can't take care of it anymore."

Might as well say my lines. "What is there to take care of?"

He shakes his head. "Way up there in those hills. I can't drive up there anymore to take a look and see if . . ."

"You don't need to take a look. It's not going to go anywhere." Then, a sudden inspiration. "Sure, let's take a look. I'll drive you up there." A ride, a walk through the grass, a change of scene might be good for him. I start to rise, but he sits still, his head now shaking with annoyance. He is not going anywhere. That's not what he wants.

"Even the weeds . . . what if the county says I have to cut the weeds? They have these fire laws now."

"We can hire someone to cut the weeds. Has the county sent you a notice?" The answer is no, or Flora would have told me.

"Can't keep paying those taxes."

"Yes, you can. They're not high."

"There's a woman says she can get me a good price."

"You mean that agent who bought your other lot? She cheated you, Dad, sold it a month later for double what she

34

paid you. While Mom was alive, she didn't have the nerve to come back again." The phone rang the day after my mother's death notice appeared. Vultures gathering.

"She says . . ." He pauses to make the most of his stunning announcement. ". . . she can get me thirty thousand."

"It's worth at least three times that," I answer, and he turns away from me, frowning, putting this statement among what he began to call "another of your smart theories" thirty years ago when he learned I had voted Democratic. "Dad, Flora told you, land on that hill has gone way up. They build mansions there now. That lot was the best investment you ever made. Leave it alone till you've spent all the money in the bank. Then sell the lot."

He shakes his head at my madness. He has no intention of subtracting, only of adding new numbers to the ones Flora adds up every week.

When both Amy and Joe had gone away to college, I put my equity in our house down on my little four-flat building. Friends were mystified. "A low-rent fixer-upper! You're free now and still young. Take a year off. Travel! You come back to a tenured job, rent a nice little apartment." I can travel later, I told them, and Joe and Amy need some help, and . . . apologetically, even sheepishly, I confessed my ineradicable immigrant psychology, the necessity to own something tangible, a piece of the land, something real "for my old age." When did my father's reality change and become numbers in a bank book?

"She's coming tomorrow with the papers."

"Dad, don't sign anything without talking to Flora and Amy!" I reply by reflex before the doubts process through my brain. Is the agent really coming? Is he playing an old tape from six months ago? I too am playing an old, obsolete tape. Let her come. Let him sign anything he wants to sign. Let her

35

close in on him, wheedling, tempting his lust for numbers. Let her put hours of work into her scheme and then find out that her efforts were for nothing. His signature is worthless without ours.

"I got to sell that lot." He starts the script again, from the top.

I don't answer.

"It's costing me . . . the taxes . . . what if I have to go up there and cut the weeds? I can't keep an eye on it."

I refuse to speak my lines.

"I can get thirty thousand for it. This woman called . . ."

Why are all the predators women? Is he just more susceptible, less wary with women?

"You know, I miss your mother so much." He breaks my wall of silence, shifts to lines I must answer.

"I know, Dad."

"We were so happy. Fifty-five years. All our hard work, and just when we had everything so perfect, just starting to enjoy . . ."

"Mom had been sick for a long time, Dad."

He nods. "She was never strong. She never got a good start. Her folks weren't much good, you know. When I took her away from them, I think she'd never had a decent meal, so skinny. Her father beat her. When he saw me coming around, he was afraid to lose her money. Eighteen, and she was supporting the whole family! My folks didn't like it either. They knew her family from the old country, 'no good, don't get mixed up with them.' But I told them, I love that girl, Pa, I love that girl. I even cried, I admit it. And your *nonna* said, 'Well, all right, you're twenty-five, old enough to know what you want.' So I brought her home."

This tape never includes my mother's memory of how grudgingly his family took her in, this thin, nervous, over-

36

educated girl whose mother was a tramp and whose father was a brute. My mother never forgave the "wedding gifts" from his family, personal gifts to him, a tie, a shirt. "Maybe they didn't know any better," I said. "They knew better," she said flatly. I judged my mother wrong not to forgive and forget. My gentle *nonna*, as far as I could see, treated her like a daughter. Now I realize that "as far as I could see" might not be very deep. Tone and look and word, inscrutable to children, can signal deathless old attitudes and relations. "Well," I smiled and shrugged at her, "you two were in love so it didn't matter." Her silence tore an even larger hole in my father's story of romantic love and rescue. That was his version, not hers, of What Really Happened.

I told my son that my mother, who carried our family life like a cross, was probably a natural born spinster. "Oh, you don't know," Joe said. "When Grandma ran away from her father, she should have moved into an apartment with a girl friend, had a little fun and got over the effects of that abuse; a few years later she would have been ready to meet some nice guy and live happily ever after." A series of sensible, casually proposed impossibilities for an Italian-American daughter of her generation or, for that matter, of mine.

"We were so happy. Why did it have to happen? We had everything we wanted and then . . ."

No, you had everything you wanted, wanting so little. She had her pain and you, your scrambled mind.

"Fifty-five years!" Outrage sharpens his voice. "We worked so hard, and then . . ." He slams his fist down on the table.

And then what? Did you think hard work earned immortality? You have always talked about the ways you were cheated, never about the misfortunes you have escaped. You escaped having to fight in two world wars. You escaped the black lung that killed your father. You have never been ill at all. You have never lost a child. You don't know what it is to live waiting for a fever or a rash to announce the beginning of your son's death!

His rage is contagious. Why do I want to attack him with rational arguments? Grief is not rational. Old age is never expected. I know that from my own shocked disapproval of the wrinkles and lumps invading my body.

"I thought I'd go first, six years older. But I think," he brightens a little, "I might make it to ninety."

I nod. How strongly he clings to this life he calls ruined, empty, frightening, a shred of a life. That must be why the numbers in his bank books are vital; increasing them adds substance, weight. Vital signs.

"What time is it?"

"Ten forty-five."

"What time is my test?"

"Four."

He sighs, looks toward the recliner chairs near the television, then remembers an alternative. He brightens. "Want to take a look at the garden?"

I almost jump out of my chair with willingness, with relief. Anything to delay the time when we will lean back into the loose folds of vinyl in that close little corner. "Sure, let's."

I follow him through the laundry room, where he again snatches his green straw hat from the hook above the washing machine.

"I think that hat has about had it, Dad."

He examines the frayed, shredded brim, the greasy, crushed crown, then silently perches it on his head. The defiant way he cocks it rebukes me. Why should he give up this familiar shape, molded to his head? Why lose one more comfort? The excitement of the new is for the young. The old need softer, cozier pleasures.

Outside on the patio, we stand still a moment blinking in the bright sunshine. I used to love this garden. I felt on safe ground here, especially after my divorce when, in the midst of what seemed a relaxed, casual conversation, my mother's fears for me would erupt in sudden anger, in the bitter reminder that "your family comes first, not all these . . . ideas," and then in her tears and my silent withdrawal, one step further, beyond reach. The garden was the one place where I never stumbled onto the wrong subject from the wrong side. When do you plant lettuce? What variety of tomato grows so large? Who taught you grafting? There were no hidden hazards in talking about plants.

"Should get another good persimmon crop this fall." The tree near the back door is thick with leaves already yellow at the edges. He does not water much back here, either.

Until her last year, my mother baked rich, black persimmon pudding-cakes, presenting them to family and friends at Christmas. When she could no longer bake, she gave me the fruit and the recipe, but I never made a good pudding-cake. The painstaking preparation made me impatient. I tried short cuts, got poor results, gave up, gave the fruit away. I am the wrong person, the wrong generation of women to take pride in this art. Amy—who has never cooked daily meals while juggling study and work and children—sees the recipe as a pleasant challenge, and plans to try it next Christmas, that is, if my father gives her any persimmons. Last winter he loaded all of them into the freezer, insisting he would thaw and eat them throughout the year. The hoard sits there, hard and dry, untouched.

He stops at the edge of the patio, at the lettuce and onion bed, dry and bare except for a struggling wild shaft of chard shredded by snails. "Almost time for another lettuce planting."

"How long does it take to get a crop?" I ask. There has been no lettuce for three years. The lettuce bed, my mother's pet, was the first to go.

"Four or five weeks, all year round. Pick it young, melts in your mouth."

He steps off the patio onto one of the planks set down last winter to bridge muddy puddles, now become chunky dirt, hard and dry as rocks. He is headed straight for a low, thick tree branch that would knock him to the ground if he did not (as I know he will) duck automatically, an inch from collision. I follow him, ducking other branches propped up by sticks as we step from plank to plank among the trees. Until a few years ago, only the two high-yielding plum tree branches were propped up, unpruned. Now all seven trees—apple, apricot, fig, plums—stretch out gnarled limbs resting on crutches. "Want some apples? They're a little wormy but good for applesauce."

True, six years ago, when he still occasionally sprayed. Now the worms have won. Apples are black at the core before they ripen. Rotten, half-formed fruit litters the ground.

"Sure." I walk the plank back to the patio to get a box, and return to start picking up fruit from the ground. Even if I fill only one box—to empty into the garbage at home—I will have managed some clean-up. But, as usual now, he stops me after I have thrown a dozen apples into the box.

"Wait a minute now, save some for your sister. And her kids too, they all like fruit." When they come, he will say, "Save some for Pat," and will hoard all but a few plums. I dread seeing what I will find next time I open his freezer.

For nearly twenty years, the bounty of this garden was laid in dozens of flats and presented to daughters and grandchildren, neighbors and friends, with deserved pride, especially the tomatoes. Thick and heavy as grapefruit, wine-red, shiny skin tight on firm, juicy meat. "Don't want to lose my reputation for growing the best tomatoes in California," he always said, grinning as he handed them to me like a tray of huge rubies. No, I can't bear to look at the tomato vines, not yet.

"My beans have about gone to seed, Dad, and I've promised the seeds to five or six more neighbors." Even in the tiny, foggy strip of ground behind my apartment, a few vines climb up four poles and manage to put out pods. A dozen of my friends grow the hardy, crisp, flat beans descended from the handful of seeds my father carried from Italy seventy years ago. I try to comfort my father with news of this dispersal, but I have only reminded him that he has none of the ancestral beans in his own soil this year. He shrugs, shakes his head, looks vaguely toward the place, near the tomato bed, where he used to grow them.

We move toward the opposite corner of the garden, where the four-plum tree sprawls over the fence and onto a neighbor's shed. I see that one of the old, over-laden branches has broken, its fruit withered; it has dwindled to a three-plum tree. "It's amazing how you grafted this, Dad. Four different kinds of plums on one tree!" He nods, smiles faintly, agreeing that skills like his are not easily acquired. When he was young he taught himself carpentering, painting, wiring, plumbing. Apart from a year of automotive school, he was a self-taught mechanic, handy with all machines. He used to roam the town dump and bring home castoff power tools, got them all working. He invented a motorized cheese grater and other funny, useful devices.

Last year, one of my advanced students (a businessman from Verona) wrote a paper titled "Northern Italians in California." Why, he wondered, were there so many here so early in the century? Why had they not stopped on the East

Coast like most of their southern countrymen? He asked my opinion. Why did they keep moving westward? Because they could, I suppose. They had industrial as well as farming skills. They could work their way across the country, could—if they were like my father—fix cars and graft trees and build tables and make wine and tear down a motor and wire up a radio.

"Want some tomatoes? I got to keep up my reputation for growing the best tomatoes in California."

I can no longer avoid the sad results of our attempt to follow Doctor Rayman's orders, "Get him back out in his garden." During the spring of my mother's death, we finally saw the truth. He was not just too depressed to work in the garden, he was lost there, had literally been losing ground for years. The talk of repairing the tiller, spraying, pruning, planting, had been little but talk long before my mother's death. Everything was beyond his control, everything except his ability to refuse our help.

Finally, help was grudgingly accepted. Teddy was allowed to turn over the impacted soil with his power-tiller. Joe and Mark were allowed to weed and fertilize the tomato bed. Flora's older daughter Jennie brought eight tomato plants, planted by her twelve-year-old Bobby. Amy hammered into the soil the thin stakes that would support the growing vines. "Okay, Grandpa, you take it from here."

We stand beside the tomato bed, the frame of supporting sticks empty above the blackened stems, sinking into the damp earth, barely sprouted at their death weeks ago. Every week I come out here to listen as he says, "Slow this year," and to wonder what went wrong, what made them go limp, stop growing, turn black?

"Too bad. No tomatoes left. Franny took them all."

"Who?" I want to force him to make eye contact with me and say it again.

"Franny, Teddy's wife. They came by last week and before they left, she came back here and helped herself."

"Franny." I watch his expression, looking for a sign of doubt or deceit. Nothing. The phantom tomatoes are harvested into his memory.

"Yep. Sorry, none left for you."

An interesting confabulation, one that nicely reflects and feeds family attitudes. Flora's new daughter-in-law accuses her of favoring Jennie's son over Franny's from a previous marriage. Jennie's response is to refuse Flora's invitations to dinner if Teddy's wife is to be there. Teddy reacts by refusing to speak to his sister, but he and his wife quarrel constantly, publicly. The days of this marriage are numbered, and no one in the family will regret its demise. Have they all prepared the way for the invention of Franny's tomato theft? My father's sister telephoned me, outraged, to ask if Franny really stripped the plants. "How could she, Aunt Eva? How could Franny take tomatoes that never existed? I don't know what happened. He even watered them without a fight. They died anyway. No tomatoes. So he tells himself they already grew and were picked. How could you believe anyone took them? Did you ever see any tomatoes?" I should not be so harshly logical with Aunt Eva. He is her "big brother," who carried her on his hip when he shot marbles with the other boys outside the mines where their fathers worked, emerging black and bitter and sick. Her big brother, who was so smart with machines he got an above-ground job at fifteen. His confusion must be more frightening and heartbreaking to her than to any of us.

Amy solved the mystery of the tomato plants. "He poured kerosene on them, Mom. I came by when he was in the garden. He was pouring from this little can, 'just a drop of something in water to kill the bugs,' he said, but it was the wrong can. I told him, 'It's kerosene, Grandpa, can't you smell it?'"

No, he can't. He has kept his teeth and all his senses except his sense of smell. Flora has nightmares about him poisoning himself with spoiled food.

"Yep, all gone, some as big as my fist. "You'll have to wait for the second crop."

"Okay, Dad." Why not? There is no reason why non-existent tomatoes shouldn't grow twice, or produce all year round for that matter. "That sun's getting really hot. We'd better go back inside."

"Time for my test?"

"No, Dad. Not till four. It's about eleven."

"That long?" He shakes his head and sighs.

"That long." I lead the way back into the house.

"Time for coffee. Want some?"

"No thanks, Dad." I take the tea kettle from the stove, reach over to the sink, pour some water into it, then set it on the stove, turning the electric dial.

In quick, almost panicky reaction, he reaches past me, snatches the kettle and, weighing it in his hand, shakes his head at my folly. He pours some of the water out into the sink, then puts the kettle back on the stove. Is he intent on saving electricity or rebuking me for not doing things correctly, as he has always done them, heating no more, no less water than he needs?

He remembered to put the kettle on a small, back coil, not one one of the two coils that wore out—how long before my mother's death? Buying and plugging in replacements, we explained over and over when we discovered the problem, was simple. We could stop at the hardware store near the supermarket. "Next time," he said, always next time. One way or another he has resisted us all this time, and since there seemed to be so many other emergencies, it hardly mattered that he had only two coils to warm his simple food. Now we know how to overcome—no, to slide past—his resistance. Flora has already bought new heating elements and will install them, a "gift" when she comes.

I am reminded of my most recent "gift." I ask, "How's the new water heater working, okay?"

He shrugs, reminded of the patience with which he endures my meddling.

I noticed during my mother's last hospital days, when I stayed here overnight, the few inches of hot water trickling out for my bath. Such inconveniences were forgotten in her death, in the sudden avalanche of needs pouring from my father. Rosetta called me last month to tell me the water heater was leaking. "He gets mad when I say this old water heater no good, how can I wash clothes?" I thanked her, promised to take care of it.

The next week, I went down on my knees, felt the damp floor, wondered why there was no puddle spreading across the washroom floor. I flashed a light underneath the tank and discovered a small hole, neatly drilled in the floor, through which water could drain beneath the house. Wait, give him the benefit of the doubt; perhaps the hole had been drilled as a safety precaution when he installed the water heater. But the little dam of wooden baseboard trim, the four pieces of wood nailed in a square wall surrounding the water heater— those were no more than a few months old. The water heater had been feeble and failing before my mother died; when had it begun to leak as well?

Of course, he did not call a plumber. He has never called

a plumber in his life. Yet he knew that finding, repairing, installing another old water heater is beyond him now. So he did what he has always done—he improvised from his resources, however reduced. He built a little dam to contain the puddle of water that might spread faster than it could drain through the little hole. He covertly wiped up the dampness and denied its existence.

When I confronted him with Rosetta's complaint, with the wet evidence, he denied, argued, forbade me to do anything—until I insisted on "giving" him a new water heater, "an early birthday present." Then the fierce denial collapsed, that terrible covert smile twisted his mouth, and he let me have my way.

The kettle starts to whistle, shrilling as it must have screamed through the house when my mother lay helpless in bed. She complained that he would start the kettle, then go out into the garden and forget it. He went on puttering, hearing neither the kettle's shrilling nor her calls with his still keen ears. Was he confabulating an earlier, happier time when she could take care of all the details he forgot?

The whistling stops as he picks up the kettle, carefully turning off the electric dial. He used to have his cup of coffee at the supermarket every day at this time. The store provided hot water, instant coffee, sugar and milk. He stood sipping with other shoppers, chatting, his only quarter hour of sociability during the day, said my mother, before he bought groceries and drove home. More than ten years ago the free coffee was discontinued. If people scattered to coffee shops nearby, my father did not join them. He took his pre-shopping coffee at home, duplicating the way he had drunk it at the supermarket: standing, sipping instant coffee from a paper cup fitted into a plastic holder whose handle was a ring just big enough for his index finger. The cracked plastic is wound around with rubber bands to keep it from falling apart.

"I need another of these plastic things. See how the paper cup fits in there? You could look around and find me one."

I shake my head. "I've looked all over. I think they only sell them by the hundreds at wholesale restaurant suppliers."

He shakes his head. "I only need one." His resentful tone says that I always misunderstand and complicate things.

"Where did you get that one?" I ask, as I have asked dozens of times.

He is puzzled, no longer prompt with the answer—another bit of his life he is losing.

"Mom used to say," "I prompt him, "you got them in Reno, brought them back from the motel. I've never found one in a store." And I really have searched, wanting to satisfy him for once, to bring him something he really wants instead of things I think he ought to want. So has Flora. So has Aunt Eva, who bought him a bright red plastic mug with a big handle, not realizing that he wanted nothing but this special kind of hollow plastic ring. When the red mug joined the dozens of other cups in the cabinet and he began asking again, she was furious. "He forgets everything—why can't he forget that stupid plastic thing?"

"I used to get my coffee free at the supermarket."

I nod. He looks at me expectantly, so I add, "Yes."

"Then they stopped. It was all those black people taking everything, pouring out all the milk for their kids, stealing the sugar. The blacks ruined it."

I am thrown off balance, as if he has suddenly tripped me, shoved me. What blacks? I see few dark faces at the supermarket or anywhere nearby. I watch him silently. Years ago, some kind of protest would already have burst from me. Like the time—twenty years after the war—when he suddenly defended the imprisonment of our Japanese-American neighbors, saying, for the first time, that he'd always feared the "yellow gangs." Like the time he agreed with Governor Reagan that Mexicans were suited to field labor because they were "built closer to the ground." (I had countered, "How tall are you, Dad, five-foot-four?") Like the time he furiously turned off a TV drama about slavery, declaring, "We were slaves, too!" glaring at my sympathetic nod, a gesture of assent not to be trusted.

Yet a black couple had lived next door to my parents for a few years, and I learned about them only shortly before they moved away again. There had been no agonizing about property values, no efforts to stop them from moving in, no ugly attempts to drive them out, no complaints, nothing. My father gave them plums and tomatoes and gardening advice, as he gave to all the neighbors. This, I knew, was the real test of racism, and my parents had passed it. I stopped challenging his racial slurs, and, when I stopped reacting, he gradually fell silent too.

Why has he suddenly attacked blacks again? No, attacked me. No, attacked the passionate—self-righteous?—girl I was, the girl who disrupted family gatherings with "those crazy ideas you picked up at college." I am shaken because he arouses that girl for an instant, a flicker of outrage before I remind myself that he is a lonely, frightened old man. But it is more than the flashback that shakes me. It is the suspicion that he is needling me, purposely evoking anger that must be blocked, swallowed, not released at an old man who can't be held responsible for what he says.

Wait a minute, what paranoid scenario am I creating out of one off-hand racial slur surfacing in the debris of his muddy memory? Is senile dementia catching? How could he be that cunning when he cannot even remember what he said five minutes ago?

He drops his paper cup into the garbage pail, then turns to the sink to place the cracked plastic cup neatly beside the jar of instant coffee. I notice something unfamiliar behind the faucet. A large cake of soap? No, a block of wood about five inches long wedged between the faucet and the formica back splash. "What's this?" I pull it out.

He gasps, leaps forward to grab the block of wood from me. I see what it was for. Water puddles up at the base of the faucet. He wedges the block of wood behind it again, and the leak slows. I open the doors below the sink and see a bucket under the pipe, which also is leaking. The bucket is placed with precision, to catch both leaks, the one from the pipe under the sink and the one from the faucet above and behind it. "Looks like you need new washers, maybe a new joint in this pipe."

"No, the pipe is fine. It'll stop. A couple of days, then I take the wood out, and it'll stop. They all do that when . . ."

He speaks with such casual assurance that I almost believe in the wooden-block method of repairing leaky plumbing. Has he really used this wedge before? No, Flora would have noticed. Probably he needs a whole new faucet. It must be replaced before the pressure of that block of wood breaks a pipe and hot water (very hot, now that we've replaced the water heater) bursts forth, flooding everything, burning him as he tries but can't remember how to turn the water off at the valve below, and . . . so I have another disaster scenario to add to the ones we imagine each time we leave him. Another long battle against his determination not to buy . . . no, now I can make him a gift of a new faucet. No need to contradict him. Let it go. Make a note to call the plumber.

"What time is it?"

"Look at the clock!"

He flinches, surprised as I am by my outburst, blinks, glances up at the wall. His distance vision without glasses is better than mine with my glasses. His voice quivers as he says. "Eleven-fifteen?"

I nod.

"And . . . my test? I'm sorry I make you mad at me, but sometimes I can't seem to remember . . . what time is my test?"

I sigh, defeated, weary, and yes, guilty. "Four."

"Those jokers, who do they think they are?" His fearful diffidence vanishes, and he is defiance itself. "I been driving for sixty years, before they were born, on dirt roads in the mountains where there wasn't even . . ."

"You know," I interrupt with sudden cunning, "it wouldn't hurt to stop at the barber on the way to the supermarket." A way to use his anxiety about the test. A way to use up time.

He feels the back of his neck, the long, straight fringe reaching under his collar, blending into his furry, curling body hair, abundant like a silver aura. He used to joke about having hair everywhere but where he needed it. "You think I need a haircut?"

I wait silently. If I say he does, he will insist it can wait another week.

"Maybe I better look good and trim when I go for my test."

"That's right." I smile, ridiculously pleased by my petty victory. "Might as well have everything going for you."

"Where's my shopping list?" He turns back to the sink. On the counter next to the bread box, a dozen scraps of paper two or three inches long, cut from old invoice forms, are stapled together. My parents sold their shop over twenty years ago. Is this supply of forms inexhaustible? Where does he keep it? When does he cut up these scraps? He tears off the top scrap, holds it at arm's length, squints, then reads, "bread

. . . cookies . . . sweet pickle relish." The list is never longer than three items, more often only one, so that he can drive to the supermarket in the morning, then again in the afternoon. Something to do, a place to go. I have never seen "gas" on his list, yet he has never run out of gas, or never told me if he did. He puts the list into his shirt pocket.

I step into the hall and call, "Rosetta, we're off to the store. You'll lock up when you leave?"

Rosetta stands in the doorway to the bathroom. "Sure, okay. *Ciao!*"

"*Mille grazie.* See you next week."

Instead of offering any thanks or farewell, my father frowns and mutters. Rosetta sees his look, shrugs, and disappears into the bathroom. Better remind him that he needn't keep trying to get rid of her, that she costs him no money. "I already paid Rosetta, Dad. You don't have to stay home to pay her when she's done. She'll just lock up and leave. Come on, let's go before the barber closes up for lunch."

He leads the way, quick-stepping through the laundry room and putting on his hat.

I follow him along the side of the house and across the driveway. He turns toward the truck.

"We'll take my car, Dad."

He stops at the end of the driveway to look into the mailbox—empty—then meekly gets into my car on the passenger side.

"Seat belt, Dad."

He grunts as he reaches for it, nods. "Your car squawks if I don't," he remembers.

51

I nod. My old car was one of the first with seat belts as standard equipment. A self-righteous buzzer, set off by the weight of a rider, nags until his belt is fastened, otherwise my father would never use the belt. The disdain of my cautious father for seat belts divides his generation from mine as clearly as anything else. What divides my generation from the next? Overdue books? Mark ran up seventeen dollars in library fines, returned the books but ignored the fines. His bright, feverish eyes flashed as he teased me, "Don't worry, Pat, I'll beat this rap. They'll never catch me where I'm going." Joe laughed insistently, until I joined in.

I start the car.

"Got to watch this street. They go pretty fast."

I glance at the road, find it empty, ease forward.

"Okay, you can go now."

I drive west one block.

"No, no, turn here!"

I silently continue west, ignoring the side street he always uses.

"Well, I guess you can turn up the next one." He shrugs, tolerant but disapproving as usual. During my mother's final hospital stay he began to let me drive him around, following his directions along tortuous, twisting routes of little side streets, routes he had mapped out in his mind years ago when they were free of traffic, little but roughly paved tracks between orchards. Now some of them are jammed with cars, less safe than wider, direct roads. But he still follows them the way some migratory birds struggle along routes where safe places of rest and refreshment have disappeared under human traffic.

"Not too fast now! They really watch you here."

I am going twenty.

"There's an arterial coming up."

I make the stop, waiting for one car crossing on my left. "Watch out for that car!"

I nod.

"Careful, the limit is twenty-five here."

I used to tell him politely that his instructions distracted me and were not necessary. He would nod, assent, and keep silent for about ninety seconds before beginning again. So I gave up. I try to ignore him. Impossible. I keep my lips pressed together, feel my jaw beginning to ache, try to loosen it while keeping my mouth shut. Last week, taking him to the doctor, I lost control, snapped at him to "keep quiet and let me drive!" then almost drove through a red light.

This week I will calm my churning gut by analyzing his nagging. In the passenger seat, my mother's seat, he becomes my mother, who read signs for him, directed turns, called red lights and green, warned of cross traffic. She directed his driving as she managed their shop, kept business and household accounts, wrote all checks and letters, made and answered all phone calls, remembered birthdays, made appointments and reminded him to keep them. When I was a child, I believed he had patiently adapted to her anxious, nervous management, as he had adapted to the restricted use of her compulsively cleaned and polished house.

Later I realized that no adaptation had been necessary. The two of them fit together into a relation I once described by blurting out to someone, "Italian men are either brutes or boys," by which I meant that my grandfathers were brutal; their sons inherited only their habit of decision-making authority. In character they were passive, like their mothers, with the same deeply hidden, unreachable streak of stubbornness. They married smart Italian-American girls, interpreters between two cultures, girls who in a way resembled their harsh fathers, quick, angry girls who vowed they would never be martyrs to their husbands' rage as their mothers had been. Instead they were martyrs of competency, of accomplishment, of duties: cleaning and cooking perfectly while holding down a job; nurturing and training well-behaved children; managing all earnings, the better to carry out, or compensate for, their husband's decisions; asking nothing from a man but that he be gentle and faithful: a good boy.

"Don't try to run that yellow light!"

As if I ever have.

"Intersection's too wide, you'd never make it across all this traffic. Up the next corner there's a light."

There is another dimension to my father's back-seat driving. He was the sole driver in our home. Women did not drive. Cars belonged to men, who made jokes about "women drivers." He gave lessons to my mother, who went rigid at the second intersection, then collapsed in tears, never to touch the wheel again, too "nervous" to drive. He gave lessons to Flora, who somehow never progressed to readiness for her test until long after she had left home. When my turn came, he took me out on a deserted country road, to drive endless, useless miles with no practice in starting, stopping, turning, shifting—until both of us were bored and sleepy, and I remained "not ready for traffic." After I married, Tony reluctantly took over, suddenly taut and grim, his habitual easy-going cheer, his avowed respect for my intelligence, lost in a contagious lack of confidence.

One furious day I read through the Driver's Manual, strapped Amy into the car bed with a full bottle, went to the motor vehicle office, passed all tests, wrested my license from those unwilling male hands. My fury dissolved in amiability and congratulations; it might even have been my father who drove me to take my test.

Yet I have never felt that assured, male ownership of the

road. Has all that changed for Amy's generation? Driver Education in the schools, women on the highway patrol. Yet it seems to me that the driver who refuses to wait for me to walk across a street or who accelerates through a yellow light is invariably a young, iron-faced woman. Not assurance, only more anger.

"Get over in the left lane so you can cross with the light!"

"Not crossing yet, Dad." When I drive, he shows total awareness of everything happening on the road before us, behind us, on all sides. The opposite of his dreamy drifting with my mother as fearful navigator. If he were only half so aware when he is driving . . .

"What are you stopping here for?"

"Remember, we're going to the barber first." I point, and he turns to look at the old-fashioned red and white pole. The stripes don't spin around anymore. These relics are turning up in antique shops now. The narrow little shop is a leftover from earlier times, sitting across the crowded boulevard from the shopping mall.

A screen door opens to a checkerboard floor, two old leather chairs, and two barbers my age, one of them Italian-American, probably the son of the man who used to cut my father's hair. The place is empty. One of the men motions my father to a chair, wraps him quickly in a sheet. I sit on a narrow red vinyl and chrome chair against the wall and pick up a *LIFE* magazine. I have not seen the inside of such a place for more than twenty-five years, not since I took Joe to his first haircuts.

"Trim around the neck?"

"Yeah. And don't charge me extra just because you have to hunt for hair to cut." All three of them laugh comfortably. Is this an habitual joke? Flora would know. Only she has been able to get him to the barber before now.

The unoccupied barber, seated high on his chair with a newspaper, says, "Looks like the price of gas is going up again."

My father makes an exasperated grunt. "I started out managing a gas station before I went into auto parts. Pump gas, clean the windshield, check the oil, tires, water, give directions, clean up after them in the toilet, all for a few pennies net. Now you pay an arm and a leg for those jokers to sit in a booth while you pump your own gas!"

"And what about repairs? If I told you what I paid for a brake job last month . . ."

"Got to keep the old car going. Who can afford the new ones?"

"All foreign makes too. I don't know, I used to say buy American, but . . ."

"Those Japanese, they know what they're doing. Who really won the war, eh?"

"Not afraid of a little work, that's why. Trouble with this country, nobody wants to do a day's work anymore. I'd like to see them put in some of the hours I used to."

"And take home nothing. Overhead kills you. Lucky I own this building."

"It's rough on the little guy. You work twice as hard."

"Try telling that to some of these kids. They say, 'You're your own boss.' Sure, you're your own boss, and you drive yourself like a slave."

The three men toss the ritual phrases with ease, my father never missing a catch or a throw, never repeating himself, never vague. His eyes have brightened, his face is lifted out of its usual depressed droop. These barbers see a man, old but vigorous, alert, aware. I watch him with a growing tightness in my mid-section. How capable and normal he looks and sounds, much as he seemed to me before my mother died. I saw no sign of the quirks she complained of. I never heard him repeat a question or a weird confabulation, never saw him go through aimless motions of forgotten chores, never heard him agree and then reverse himself a moment later. When my mother compressed her lips and flashed angry looks at him, I thought the illness of her old age had brought back the chronic anger I remembered from my childhood, now directed at him instead of at me and Flora.

My jaw is freezing up again. I must be glaring at him as she did. I must be asking myself the same question she asked herself. Why is he lost, infantile, confused with me and then suddenly capable and sharp with strangers? Why does he never ask a stranger the same question over and over again?

Probably if he were here with these two men for half an hour, his "normality" would begin to slip. He would repeat a question or a part of the ritual conversation, interject a disconcerting confabulation or an irrelevant recollection. Is that why he refuses to see old acquaintances, meet new people, not because "It's no fun without your mother" but because he knows he cannot make sense for long? No, no, he repeats and confabulates because he forgets and therefore is too muddled to know he is muddled. Yet he has some control, makes some choices. What choices? What Really Happens?

"Five dollars." The barber peels off the sheet, turning toward his tray of clippers and combs. Suddenly my father's face collapses into confusion. He is looking at me, hopelessly lost. I see him above the pages of my magazine, but I pretend not to. I want to jump up, to repeat the price, to explain that he must pay, to pay the man myself, to be a competent, managing, good daughter. I pretend to be engrossed in finishing an article. I am determined to wait, to see what will happen without me. It's not easy. I grip the magazine so hard that I rip the page. I grip the vinyl seat with tense thighs. One by one, I loosen each muscle, make my fingers, arms, legs, relax, let go. I wait.

Slowly my father eases himself down from the chair. He stands looking around uncertainly.

"Five," the barber repeats, turning to him with a smile.

The soft grunt that comes from my father's throat is the same as the one he made at the mention of the rising price of gas. It is accusing and resigned, full of irony and injury. Has the barber's smile turned ironic too? Does he exchange a quick glance with the other barber? Or do I only imagine I see it?

My father's hand moves in slow motion down to his back pocket and slides his wallet out. His fingers explore the wallet and slowly count the dollar bills into the barber's hand. "One . . . two . . . three . . . four . . . " He hesitates as if he cannot grip the last one. ". . . five." He would not dream of tipping, Flora tells me, a great embarrassment to her.

I tell her she should not feel embarrassed, that the people who serve my father in shops and banks and gas stations are used to old people who are slow, need more help, and who always expect items to cost what they did forty years ago. But, as I put down my magazine and follow my father to the door, I realize that I am sweating, and it's not that hot yet.

"Watch out! A lot of cars coming."

More than a block behind us. I ease the car away from the curb, signal, then move into the left lane.

"You turn left up here. The light is changing. It's okay now. There's the driveway into the parking lot, up there on the side, see it?"

"Yes." I turn into the driveway and stop in the first parking stall.

"What are you stopping way out here for? There's a place, plenty of places, right up near the door."

It never works. I try to park at the outer edge, make him walk across the parking lot, sneak in a little bit of the exercise his doctor recommends. I shrug, back out of the stall.

"Turn left. No, no, all the way up. Someone just pulled out, right up near the door. Go slow here!"

The day after my mother died, when he kept slipping into denial of his loss, I insisted we take a walk, "to clear our heads, just around the block." I'm sure that was the first and last time he ever walked around the block he has lived on all these years. When I was a child, he drove his car even to the corner store to buy cigarettes. Only at rare Italian picnics did I see him take pleasure in moving for the fun of it, one-stepping around the dance platform, walking the length of a horseshoe pit.

At fourteen he was hauling sacks of coal and grain. At seventeen he walked miles to work with pick and shovel. When he said "labor-saving machine," he pronounced the words as if naming a sacred object, a miracle that preserved precious human energy, human dignity, even life itself. Exercise for its own sake is regression into slavery, almost immoral if not insane.

I pull into a stall near the door to the supermarket. My father fumbles with his seat belt. I unhitch it, and he gets out, heading toward the row of nested shopping carts. He struggles to detach one, tests it, finds it wobbly and hard to steer, pulls out another.

"We don't need this just for three items," I protest as I help him.

"Why carry them?"

"I'll carry them for you."

He ignores me and continues to search for a pushable cart.

"It's more trouble to get one and push it around—just to carry a loaf of bread." Like driving his car to the corner store to get cigarettes.

"I . . . I like to lean on it when I walk," he admits with a grimace, shaming me, silencing me. He always seems so quick and nimble, but I see him only in short sprints across his kitchen or from tree to tree in his back yard. The long supermarket aisles, the wait at the checkout stand, the hard concrete floors, the bright florescent lights, the drone of insipid canned music—all these make me tired too.

He finds an acceptable cart, pushes it onto the rubber entry mat, and the doors swing open. "Where's my list?" If he were alone would he reach for it without hesitation? Is he just making conversation?

"In your shirt pocket."

He reaches to his breast. "Oh, yeah, here it is." He squints at it. "Bread. Cookies. Sweet pickle relish." He nods, satisfied, then turns and pushes the cart slowly down a long aisle, glancing left, right, left, right, at the crowded shelves. "Let's see now, where's the cookies?" He began doing the shopping alone here fifteen years ago, during my mother's first heart episode. The layout is as familiar to him as his own house. Just conversation.

"I think the cookies are over that way, Dad. Near the bread."

I follow as he slowly turns the cart and moves to the end of the aisle, examining each shelf he passes, as if to make sure I have not misdirected him past the cookies. Probably he wants to prolong this exploration. It is becoming his only outing, his only stimulation. He turns and moves up the next aisle while I inch along behind him.

I am thrown back thirty years, to the days when Amy, then Joe, took their first steps, made their explorations of the world, and I walked slowly behind, alert to danger, resisting the temptation to do for them what they were learning to do for themselves. It took patience, but my curiosity helped, my interest in seeing how they would solve the mystery of each encounter with the new, the unknown, how they would add bit by bit to their expanding world.

Following my father down these aisles takes that same patience without the support of curiosity. I do not want to examine the process by which he uses and loses his dwindling powers in his shrinking world. I see myself in his place— thirty years from now if I last that long, please God, no—and I should feel empathy, patience, compassion, not this impotent rage smoldering in my gut. Flora was hospitalized with some kind of gastric upset last month. We will both, she says, end up with ulcers.

He finds the shelf of cookies, then the brand, MOTHERS, then, more slowly, reading label after label, his choice, MACA-ROONS. He peers through the transparent wrapping to make sure they are indeed the flat, pale, dry wheels that will not crumble when he dunks them in his wine. Finding them is a success that makes his face shine for a moment before he begins the next quest. He turns to me. "Where's my list?"

"I think the bread is on this same aisle, Dad, that way."

"Bread? Is bread on my list?"

I nod. He pulls out the list to check. Yes, he remembers where the list is. Just conversation.

The examination of bread shelves takes longer—past the rolls, muffins, the long, bright, slickly-wrapped loaves of sliced white bread, open paper bags of French bread, sealed bags of sticks, crumbs, stuffing mixes. I see a new item, a whole wheat bread I tried once when my bakery was closed. "How about some of this, Dad?"

"What?" He peers at the loaf in my hand, his arms

hanging at his sides as if he fears I might force him to take it. "I don't like that dark stuff."

"It's better for you," I shrug as I replace it on the shelf.

He makes the same grunt he gave the barber before paying him. "Eighty-two years on white bread, I'll live an extra year if I switch now?"

I laugh. "Right you are, Dad."

But he will not laugh with me. He turns away, solemnly fixes his eyes on his choice, pulls it from the shelf, glances through the wrapping, nods, places it in the cart. His choice is a pale, rounded loaf sheathed in plastic, labeled SLICED FRENCH but bearing no resemblance to the French bread we ate at home in my childhood, nor to what I now eat alternately with dark bread. I don't know how long ago he abandoned French bread for this stuff, but I finally have guessed why. Not that he could not chew the crisp brown crust—his teeth are sounder than mine—but that this bread, like the iceberg lettuce he barred from our home but uses exclusively now, lasts longer. Never tasty and fresh, never hard and stale, always the same bland, dry dough to the last slice.

He reads the last item on his list. "Sweet pickle relish." He leads the way to the other side of the store where he finds it among rows of jars with green contents. He buys a jar almost every time we come to the store. He must put it on everything, this total violation of the Italian palate, mixing sweet and sour. Why? Of course. The loss of his sense of smell. If most taste is located in the nose and only sour, sweet, salt on the tongue—for him this concoction is full of sensation.

"You need anything?"

I shake my head. I buy food in small shops, one for fresh produce, another for cheese, another for freshly baked bread. I have lived long enough to see supermarkets come and, perhaps, begin to go. The rebirth of the little shop specializing in what it does well is like a return to the best of my childhood. On one block near our old home stood the Italian delicatessen, the French bakery, the Swedish butcher. The Japanese vegetable truck came by weekly to supplement our garden produce. All these disappeared before I moved to the city, but they have been resurrected or reborn in a new version in Sequoia Park, just as they have been reborn in the city. Flora heard about the rebuilding of the old, abandoned town hall as a complex of little food shops "with really good prosciutto and fresh pasta." I suggested to my father that we explore them together, rediscover old favorite sights and smells. He was uninterested, even anxious at the suggestion of driving to an unfamiliar part of town.

As we stand in line at the check-out stand, he picks up each item from his cart and checks the price. He calculates, totals the prices in his head. He reaches for his wallet and takes out a five dollar bill, mutters more calculations, then nods his head, satisfied. He knows the total cost and how much change he should receive from his five dollars. How can he, with his memory problems, hold these figures in his head? "Well," Flora laughs when I mention it, "I guess it's because they involve money."

Did he make these calculations twenty years ago when the list was long, when he brought home bags full of groceries? No, then my mother shopped; he drove. This habit of calculating his two or three purchases, checking the checker, probably is a throwback to his childhood, new in America, where an immigrant was cheated however and whenever he could be, in the purchase of land, or the payment of wages, or the most petty, five-cent transaction.

All at once I remember a story about his father, who stood at the center of my childhood, gasping curses at God with what little was left of his miner's lungs, while he resoled my shoes on his little cobbler's bench. At some earlier, more hopeful time before my birth he bought his first radio, a large console delivered to his house. When it came, he angrily returned it, accused the salesman of trying to cheat him. It was not the one he had chosen, the one on which he had secretly made his mark so that no imitation could be substituted. He would not listen to my father's explanation of floor models and department store stock. He had been cheated, robbed, exploited in so many ways that his peasant shrewdness had become irrelevant. He had learned to trust no one, ever, and even this lesson betrayed him, made a fool of him yet again.

My father counts his change and nods, satisfied. I pick up the bag and he follows me out.

As soon as I have him buckled in, I start to talk, to head off more verbal driving from him. "Have you seen Cousin Louie? Ever go to watch the bocce ball game with him?"

He shakes his head.

"Don't they play at that park near your house? Some men your age hang out there and watch."

"I don't know any of them."

"Maybe you'd get to know some. Just walk over there and . . ."

"Naw." The sound is full of disgust—at Louie, at bocce ball, at my stupidity in suggesting such a substitute for his true need.

"At least you'd be getting out, seeing people, watching a game. Louie was lonely too after Marietta died, but then he started getting out, and . . ."

"Yeah." Heavy sarcasm. "He goes to church on Sunday too, then out to lunch with a bunch of widow ladies."

"That doesn't sound so bad. You could go along. Didn't they offer to pick you up?"

"Go along where? To church?" He stares at me, wide-eyed, as if to see if I have completely lost my wits. His stunned incredulity makes me laugh; again he refuses to laugh with me.

"I think churches are different now. The priest won't try to run your life, and I don't think you even have to kneel." He turns away, relentlessly shaking his head. I shrug, "At least you'd be with people, that's all I mean."

"I don't want to be with 'people.' I don't want much. Just my home, a little work in the garden, as long as I had your mother . . . is that so much to ask for!"

The lesson: never, never be satisfied with little. Subtracting one of few satisfactions leaves such a huge, gaping hole. Flora says we both have too many interests, too many friends, to end up this way, even if (as we both fear) the failure of his mind is something hereditary. "When we're old," says Flora, "we're just what we always were, only more so. I have friends in their eighties who are busy doing things, going places, reading ." Yes, but I had a friend in her eighties, a woman with dozens of interests and friends. She died last month after a four-year deterioration to a moaning, hallucinating skeleton. Parkinson's Disease. Nothing buys immunity.

"I told you what I need," he insists. "Just someone to stay with me. She could have free rent, just cook a little and clean up. She'd have her own room. Free rent and food."

"When Amy stayed with you, she bought all the food, and then you told her she owed you rent." He shakes his head, amazed that I could invent such a story. I can hardly believe it myself.

65

Amy, in transit between apartments, agreed to stay a month with her vague, gentle, lonely grandfather, in whom she too discovered a man she had never known. During that month my telephone sounded the alarms twice as often, most of the calls from my usually cool, competent Amy, a slow crescendo of hysteria. "He won't let me out of the kitchen, won't let me use the dining room table if I bring home work, won't let me do anything but sit in Grandma's chair and watch TV with him. So I sit and he doesn't say a word, doesn't even look at me, falls asleep. But if I pick up a book or a brief, he's awake and at me, saying the same thing over and over and over. He's not satisfied just to have company, Mom, he has to invade my mind. I can't have my own thoughts."

"Amy went out and left me alone at night," he remembers.

"A young woman won't stay home every night, Dad."

"That's the worst time. Dinner time and after."

Yes, I know. It's true for me too. The hard part of living alone at any age. To come home from work, and there's no one to tell about the day's battles, lost or won. No listener to help you sort out What Really Happened. To feel tired and want to stay at home with a good book, but not completely alone, just someone breathing in the next room. Friends are good. Neighbors are friendly. But not the same as someone at home, just breathing in the next room. No point in telling my father this by way of commiseration; to him, my living alone is my fault, my choice, not a misfortune like his, but a deserved punishment.

"It would be a good deal for some woman on a pension, a nice home like mine."

"Flora and I have tried and tried, Dad, you know that. Nearly all the women looking for a live-in job are minorities. Asian, Hispanic, black. I have a student, a fine woman from Indonesia, another from Peru. If you would only consider . . ."

"No, no, I mean a woman who understands English."

"They understand English."

"No, I mean a woman . . ."

"Just like Mom."

He nods, missing or ignoring the irony in my voice. "There's plenty of widows around."

"Yes, widows who nursed sick husbands till they died, and don't want . . . they prefer their own quiet little place." They don't want to be free caretakers under the rule of your stubborn senility. Amy's experience made it clear. Living with my father is a job, a hard job.

"Even that woman you got before—that Daisy. She was all right. I don't know why you sent her away."

"Dad, that's not what you said when she was living with you." Daisy, cute little Daisy even at sixty-four, always smiling and vague, the great white hope of Sequoia Park's Home Companion Reach-out. Another lesson learned: abandon all hope for help from government agencies, whose only function seems to be to dream up titles and put out brochures. The staff I dealt with turned out to be as irresponsible, indifferent, and elusive as Daisy herself. "Daisy? We've had no other complaints," probably because the only way each household could get rid of her was to give a good reference, unload her on someone else.

"She was out most nights, Dad, disappeared every weekend. She thought we'd hire her, then forget you. Remember, she cooked that huge pot of rice and left it in the refrigerator for you to eat for two weeks? She turned her bedroom into a cat kennel, and she ran up a long distance phone bill that was double the highest rent she could have paid for a house all to herself." Calls to Las Vegas and Chicago. Flora thinks Daisy must be some gangster's aging girl friend on the run. Fortunately for us, she kept running, disappeared. "And Dad, I was paying her—get that?" I have never told him this before.

67

"She was free all day. All she had to do was dinner and the evening with you six nights a week, and I paid her a salary."

He shakes his head, not disbelieving, just not interested in my folly, my mishandling of a simple problem. He would be interested if he knew I had paid Daisy with his money. "I thought you had another one. You said you did."

"You mean the one who lives with the manager of the senior center in East Honda. Her aunt, respectable, honest, easy-going, sixty years old."

"Yeah, that's the one."

"She turned out to be over seventy, recovering from a hip replacement, and when I interviewed her, I saw she was having memory problems, confusion." Like you. "Her niece was trying to dump her somewhere while she took a trip to Europe. Want to hear the latest response I got from my ad? Some woman called me yesterday, said her twenty-year-old son is unemployed and sits around watching TV all day. She didn't see why I wouldn't want him to move in and watch it with you." I laugh, but, of course, he doesn't.

"No, no," he says, shaking his head, trying to be patient with my stupidity. "What I want is a woman, some widow . . ."

"One woman I interviewed was drunk. There are plenty of those, Dad. Plenty of white alcoholics, white drug addicts in treatment programs, who'd just love to move in with you. But there aren't a lot of healthy, sober white widows who want to leave their own quiet lives to . . ."

"There is . . . this woman . . . ."

Why won't he say her name? Develia.

I stop the car and park under a tree, the shady spot Rosetta has vacated. He watches me as I unbuckle his seat belt, waits for me to go on with the old script, objecting, warning, refusing to consider admitting Develia. I say nothing, make no protest. I wait for him to go on. He decides not to. He gets out of the car and checks his empty mailbox.

"What time is it?"

"Just noon."

"Time for lunch," he says, almost cheerfully, and leads the way across the driveway and down the path.

In the kitchen again, we put the groceries away: relish in the refrigerator, bread in the polished steel bread box, cookies in the tallest of the matching cannisters. The house is quiet. Rosetta has locked up, as she promised, closing the door to the front rooms.

These walls are closing in on me.

I feel as confined as I did forty years ago in our house on the wrong side of the tracks that used to run through Sequoia Park, a house half this size, a kitchen half this size, three or four steps from sink to stove to table, my tiny corner of table where I ate, did my homework, read, listened to the radio. In that house, too, the front rooms existed only for cleaning— daily dusting, weekly vacuuming and polishing. Even the tiny bedroom Flora and I shared was forbidden during the day; our beds, the only place to sit, were expected to retain the smoothness of regulation army cots.

Our home was no different from Aunt Eva's, no different from many other proud, home-owning immigrant families. Some even covered sofas and rugs with sheets before they closed the doors and huddled in the kitchen, servants to their own houses. Some built a room in the garage, moved in a stove, an old round table, scuffed old chairs and sofa. They added shelves of playing cards and board games, a radio, a sink, a toilet, a sewing machine. Such a family might spend easy convivial days in the garage; late at night they re-entered

69

their house, tiptoed past the shrouded emblems of their prosperity, and went to bed. Our garage contained a wrecked car or two my father repaired and sold, but it would not have been converted to easy living space in any case. My parents spent their time working, at the shop or at home.

This image of our home life is incomplete, unjust, not What Really Happened. There were frequent family dinners, festive birthdays, anniversaries, holidays, when we spread throughout the house. There was my tenth birthday party, more lavish than any of my friends' annual ones. There was a piano bought for me with Depression-scarce dollars, and daily practice in the otherwise forbidden front room, and sometimes my mother listening through the open door to the kitchen while she ironed. During my year at the junior college, before I married and left, my books and papers covered the dining room table, where I studied.

But memory is never fair. These relaxations of rules fade beside images of my mother's fury at a scratch on her hardwood floors (the floors were "hers," just as the shop and the money were "his"). Any lapse, a careless word, a spill or a scrape, a forgotten step in our cleaning ritual, might trigger a long, enraged lecture ending with the reminder that I, who had never known what it meant to begin life on a dirt floor, would never comprehend the sacrifices made for me.

This is not the woman who died last year. That woman spoke gently, bore her suffering quietly, smiled her gratitude for my infrequent visits. The whole truth can be a mistake, a distortion of the here and now. I saw her, not as the weak woman she was in those last years, but like an image in a photograph obscured by multiple exposures over time: the young woman furious at the mess I was making on her floor; the middle-aged woman stricken by the mess she feared I was making of my life. My vision was always blurred by images of a relation that existed forty years ago.

One day in particular stands in my memory as symbolic of that relation. I was bathed, combed, dressed in my finest; we were going . . . somewhere, to Aunt Eva's for a holiday dinner, perhaps. Our house had been scrubbed to untouchable perfection. Even my corner of the kitchen table was forbidden. I must vacate the pristine house while my mother dressed. No, not out to the street where I might run off with friends. No, not to my toy shelf in the garage, where I would get dirty. No, not to the shady back porch, where it was cold and I would get sick again. To the back yard, but not among the freshly planted vegetables and flowers. The only place left was the foot-wide concrete walk bordering the planted beds. How long did I pace that prisoner's walk, round and round the tiny square of forbidden soil? Surely no more than half an hour.

I hate that scene, not because it happened, but because I never forgot it, let it swell up to a symbol of my childhood, a symbol that reeks of self pity. Must the child in us remain so unforgiving? Does Joe still think about the time I slapped him and, to my horror, bloodied his nose? Does Amy still announce to people, "I have a lot of allergies because my mother refused to breast-feed me"? Has either of them really, wholly forgiven me for ripping their home apart?

"Well, now, what's for lunch?" asks my father, opening the refrigerator with cheerful foreknowledge of the answer. "What's this?" He stares into the refrigerator, nearly empty but for the aluminum plate I brought.

"Captain's Plate," I remind him. "You know, that fish you like."

"Oh, yeah. Want some for lunch?"

"Let's save it for dinner." After his driving test, when he is depressed or raving, and I am too wrung out to think of cooking, we can share this plate.

He nods. "Plenty of other things for lunch," he says as we

view the nearly bare, white spaces of the refrigerator. I look at the gleaming, empty shelves gratefully. A friend's mother shops every day like my father, but lavishly, pushing and piling new containers of food onto the rotting, wilted, rancid accumulation regularly cleaned out by her daughter. Another friend (another daughter, never a son) finds colonies of mice multiplying all over her mother's house, following the shifting caches of food she hides in new places after her daughter discovers and removes them. For once I appreciate my father's frugality. I help him draw out his usual lunch food: the head of iceberg lettuce, gutted, washed, drained, and sitting whole on a plate; small, wrapped pieces of salami and cheese on a saucer; the jar of sweet pickle relish.

While I wash my pear and get the bread, he reaches under the sink and lifts out a bottle of red wine, decanted from the gallons delivered too often. He puts another paper place mat on the table, and I set out a plate, glass of water, knife, and fork for myself. Paper napkins are bunched into a metal rack on the table next to the toaster and his bottle of pills. He pauses and looks at the table, nods with satisfaction, pleased that it is properly set, pleased that it is set for two instead of only for one. We sit down.

"Want some?" he asks as he pours himself a glass of wine.

"No thanks, Dad. Too early for me."

He notices the bottle of pills, picks it up, slowly reads aloud as if for the first time, "Diaboneze. One before each meal." He nods, opens the bottle, shakes out a pill.

Until he turned fifty, my father ate hugely, sugared his wine, grew rounder and rounder. Then, diagnosed diabetic, he amazed us by his total conversion, turning forever from rich pastries and sauces, a born-again nibbler of spare, bare portions. He even quit smoking. He lost fifty pounds and never regained an ounce. Of course, it was my mother who studied the diets, weighed his food, balanced the portions, but it was his will—the iron will I have only recently realized—that made him shed his favorite indulgences when their threat to his well-being was made clear. He controlled his disease by diet alone until a few years ago. When my mother died, we worried that without her constant reminders, he would forget to take his Diaboneze. But he never forgets.

I am rising to get him a glass of water when he pops a pill into his mouth and washes it down with a gulp of wine, a health contradiction, a new development. Not so new. My mother began to complain five years ago, but I could not believe her. I still cannot believe the telltale signs, the red lines radiating from his nose: he drinks too much. Two glasses of red at lunch. Sherry before dinner "only one glass, *un dito*," but he forgets, pours that "one glass" again and again. Two glasses of red at dinner. So he says. I have seen him at his most clear and rational. From noon until bedtime at eight, he becomes more and more muddled.

He unwraps the cheese and salami, cuts a thin slice of each onto his plate, peels one leaf from the head of lettuce, pushes a dollop of relish onto his plate, then half rising, leans forward and drops two slices of bread into the toaster. He sips wine while he waits for the toast and urges me, expansively, "Help yourself, have some cheese," pointing to the withered white cube on the saucer. I'm not sure when he began buying bargain wheels of white jack, cutting it into wedges, wrapping it, freezing it. The first few wedges are not bad, but later ones, like this one, thaw out dry and hard, with half an inch of gray near the skin.

The toast pops up just out of his reach. He spears it with his cheese knife, drops one slice on his plate, one on mine. The toaster sits at the exact center of the table. Once I moved it a few inches, to put it within his reach. Next time I came, it was back at the center of the table. Spearing his toast must be fun for him, or maybe more comfortable than touching hot toast with fingertips, or . . . whatever the reason, I began to learn my lesson: let him do what he likes if it does no harm. He has rights that do not depend on my understanding.

I cut myself a piece of the dry, tasteless cheese, and I think of the cheese that hung over the wine barrels in our cellar, filling it with strong, musty smells.

I remember my mother, Saturday noon, home from the shop alone, waving Flora and me off to the four-hour matinee at the local movie house. She sat at the kitchen table with a loaf of sour dough French, a thick red salami, a high-smelling gorgonzola, the newspaper, and a smile of blissful contentment as she anticipated an afternoon of solitude.

A month after her death, when the real shock set in and I was frozen in unanticipated grief, a friend counseled me, "Think of her during a happy time." I tried. Not the harried sessions of housecleaning. Not the anxious hours behind the counter at the shop. Not the evening bookkeeping across the kitchen table from my studying, biting her lip until she "balanced." Not the festive family dinners where, exhausted after a week of preparation, she waited apprehensively, almost resentfully, for the favorable verdict on her always superb cooking. This Saturday noon scene at the kitchen table was the best, the most purely happy picture of her I could conjure up. I am not in it.

My father eats silently, neatly, precisely—a bite of cheese, of relish, of bread, a nibble from the lettuce leaf, all washed down by a sip of wine. He measures his bites so that he will "come out even." If I offer him half of my pear, he will refuse, disdaining any fruit he did not grow, stew, freeze himself. But if I silently put a piece of my pear on his plate, he will eat it with pleasure, provided I have peeled it, a typically Italian requirement. What about the lost benefits of eating the whole fruit, all the fiber and nutrients in the peeling? He would point out, justly, that he never catches cold, never has a stomachache.

He pours another glass of wine.

"Dad, do you think you ought to . . ."

"What? What's the matter?"

I look silently at the wine.

"A glass of wine with meals is good for you. Not too much. Wine is a food. Take it only as a food." He recites this explanation in the same measured tones he used forty years ago when he condemned our neighborhood drunk. He takes another sip, closes his lips delicately over a burp.

"That's your third glass."

"No! Second. Two glasses at lunch, two at dinner, never more." Is he right? Maybe it is only his second. But what he eats with it would hardly fill one glass. His face is flushed, his speech already blurring. "Got no use for people who drink too much. Drown their sorrows! Huh. Make their sorrows. Like the family in the old country when I was a little kid. Ever tell you about them?"

Yes, but I encourage him to tell me again and again. The further back he goes in memory, the closer he gets to What Really Happened. Unlike the story I read this morning, rather like a car with a faulty transmission, his mind works best in reverse. Besides, I like these stories. I should bring my tape recorder next week.

"They called those years *la miseria*, the factory shut down for months at a time, my father gone to America. My uncles sat around, drank wine, slept, woke up and started drinking again. While they slept, I used to drain all the glasses. Six years old, an alcoholic at six, it's the truth. We'd have starved if it hadn't been for *Magna* Pina."

Here comes the part of the story I like.

"My great-aunt. She used to go out every morning before dawn, all bent over, this sack on her back. Dry goods, thread, pins, lace, anything she could scrounge from the mill when it shut down—bits of cloth, ribbon. Walked the roads, past Lanzo, through all the villages, peddled whatever she could. At night she'd come home and scratch her marks on the fireplace stones. She couldn't read or write, but she kept her accounts straight, on those stones, right down to the penny. She put food on the table for all of us." He stops, looks at me, frowns, and I wait eagerly for his closing line. "You know, as you get older, you're starting to look like her."

I smile. I can't remember the last time he paid me such a compliment. If that's what it is.

"Three more years of that. Then my mother and I took the boat. She didn't want to go, didn't want to leave her family. She cried and cried, and as soon as the ship left the dock, she got sick. She was sick the whole crossing, three weeks, laying there. I thought she was dying. I kept trying to tell them, my mother is dying, but no one understood Italian, and they just smiled, and I thought, my God, these Americans, they are monsters. When we finally got here, another week on the train, and what did we find? My father drinking hard too. It was the mines, killing work. No money for food. He spent it in the saloon before he got home. Or there'd be a layoff and no money except what my mother got cooking and washing for other miners. All the men drinking even more from nothing else to do. Your Aunt Eva was born nine months after we got here. I didn't know anything. I came home from school one day, and there she was. You know what I did? I started to cry. I said, "We don't even have enough to eat, and you go out and buy a baby!" What a thing for a boy to say the first time he sees his baby sister! We used to keep a little *grappa* in a trunk in the closet, for sickness, a teaspoon for upset stomach, for the flu . . . and my mother was so weak and white as a ghost, so I went to get some out of the trunk for her. The bottle was empty. My father had even drunk the medicine! Ten years old, I looked at that empty bottle, and I said to myself, I'll never do that. After that, I never drank, only when I eat, use wine as a food."

True, I have never seen my father drunk. I never saw him do more than nurse a drink politely at a family dinner or a wedding while the other men downed glass after glass. But the incredible is undeniable. His drinking has been slowly but steadily increasing for years. Now that he is here all alone without my mother to nag restraint . . . I tell his doctor, who gazes somewhere above my head and murmurs, "Make sure he eats." How?

"Time for dessert." He gets up and goes to the sink, opens the cannister and takes out one cookie. He offers the cannister to me, but I shake my head, and he returns it to the counter. Back in his chair, he splits the hard disk exactly in half and dips one half into his wine. Silently he nibbles and sucks the wine-soaked cookie. When he starts the second half, he murmurs, "Didn't come out even," and pours more wine, peers at the bottom of the bottle, then empties it, filling his glass. "That reminds me, I have to call Bertini and order more wine."

"I thought they delivered a case just over a week ago. Don't tell me you've gone through four gallons."

He raises the glass to his lips, drinks. "I think I won't finish all of this—want to be sharp for my test." He gives me a wink of wise humor and sets the glass down. About an inch of wine, clouded with cookie crumbs, remains.

"Dad, four gallons of wine in less than two weeks—along with the sherry—that's too much for . . ."

"No, only three gallons."

"A different-sized case?" I hadn't noticed that. "Only three gallons to a case? I thought there were four."

"One was empty."

"They delivered a case with one empty gallon? Someone made a mistake?"

"They do it all the time."

"You mean Bertini is charging you for four gallons and delivering only three? How long have you been buying his wine, thirty-five years? I can't believe the old man would . . ."

"That's the way it is."

"But that winery is a huge corporation now. They only deliver to you for old times' sake, more trouble than it's worth. Why would they short you a gallon?"

"It's those new kids who deliver here on the way to the restaurants."

"You mean the trucker steals a gallon?"

He shrugs.

"Did you complain?"

He shakes his head.

"You want me to complain? I'll call them."

"No, no." His voice is panicky. "They'll take it out on me. They'll stop delivering."

"So what? There are brands of good, cheap wine on the shelf at the supermarket."

"Forget it, forget it. That's the way they are now, that's all."

How can he accept being cheated this way—after calculating every penny of change due him from every purchase at the store?

"What time is it?" He takes a toothpick from a cup beside the toaster and begins to pick his teeth, another Italian habit. Is that how he has kept all his teeth? He glances at his glass, picks it up, finishes off the remains of the wine.

78

Suddenly I realize what has happened. I have witnessed the birth of a new confabulation. The wine disappears more and more rapidly. Flora notices. I notice. We warn him, we nag, we say the unspeakable, the incredible: he drinks too much. Since our conclusion from the evidence is not acceptable, he has invented another. Empty gallons are none of his doing; they come to him already empty.

Wait until Flora hears this one. Should I forewarn her? I feel an odd impulse of mischief, to let him spring this one on her as he did on me, see what she makes of it, how long it takes her to catch on. I want to laugh. I want to grab him and shake him. I want to scream at him that old age should bring wisdom, dignity, should at least retain self-respect. Oh, is that so? Who am I to prescribe how he should face his final losses, his end? When I face mine, not so many years from now, maybe I too will decide that "wine does more than poets can to justify God's ways to man." Or is it "mead" does more than "Milton"? Is misquoting familiar poetry a sign of incipient memory loss?

"What time is it?"

"Twelve-twenty-five."

"What time is my test?"

"Four."

"Hope I don't get that same joker again. I told him all I needed was a little brake fluid, but he . . . some Mexican . . . give them a little power and they . . ."

"It will be a different examiner," I tell him, "someone who comes from the city to handle appeals."

He strokes his toothpick across his paper place mat, already stained and streaked with criss-cross tracks of food from how many toothpicks, how many meals? Years ago my parents began using these thin paper place mats, discarding them with their paper napkins after each meal, or at least by the end of the day. Since my mother's death (and how long

79

before? was this a minor queerness she didn't bother to mention?) he keeps the same paper mat day after day, fighting our attempts to change it for another from the hundreds stacked in the drawer.

I get up and begin to clear the dishes. I wait for the moment when he leans back in his chair, ready to get up, his hands off the table. Then, in one fast, casual sweep, I pick up his plate with one hand while, with the other, I snatch his place mat, crushing it into my fist so that, even as he twitches his hand forward to stop me, he sees that he has lost it to the garbage can. I feel a cheap thrill of victory over him.

But he wins the battle of the dishes this time. I don't even put up a fight. In my kitchen, plates and glasses sit all day on the sink, waiting for hot, soapy water after dinner, a practice unthinkable in my mother's kitchen. When there are too few dishes to fill the basin with hot soapy water, he insists on a tepid rinsing under the faucet. There never are enough dishes anymore for hot soapy water. Gradually the dishes, glasses, spoons, and especially forks are acquiring a dull film. One of these days, Flora says, when we are both here together, we will take piles of plates out of the cabinet and wash them properly.

He holds a dish under the tap, then hands it to me. I wipe it. Suddenly he clutches the edge of the sink, swaying.

"What is it, Dad?"

"Oh." He shakes his head. "Sometimes I just get these little dizzy spells."

After wine at lunch. After sherry at four o'clock. "Want to sit down? I'll finish."

"No, I'm all right now." He hands me the forks and knives to wipe. "You know, after we retired from the shop, your mother and I used to do this together. I miss her so much."

80

"Yes, Dad."

"We were so happy. Why did it have to happen? Just when we could . . . we always had to work so hard, and then just when we could begin to take it easy and enjoy life . . ."

"You had some very good years after you retired."

"And then all of a sudden, just when we were starting to enjoy our house, our garden, our leisure . . ."

"Mom had been sick a long time, Dad."

He pauses, nods. "That's right." He turns to look me in the face. "She was never well again after your divorce."

As I put the last dish in the cabinet, he takes one out, setting the table for his next meal: fresh paper place mat, dish, glass, knife and fork. While dirty dishes never remain on the sink, a few clean ones stand on the table ready for his next meal, day and night. He seems anxious until all are in place for the future.

Flora admits that she has begun to set her breakfast table before going to bed. "It just seems easier in the morning, to get started, you know." She giggles. "Or is senile obsessive behavior catching?" Good question. A thirty-year-old friend tells me that after a day in doctors' offices with her ailing seventy-year-old mother, she creaks along home, bereft of her usual unconscious ease, awkward and fearful of betrayal by her young body. It takes her hours to regain her normal rhythm.

"Will I have to take the written test again?"

"I think so."

"I passed the written test already!"

"The letter said you have to do both the written test and the road test."

"What letter?"

"You have all the stuff in the desk. Want to go through it again?" I step over to the desk, tilt out the hinged flap.

He jumps in front of me, hovering between me and the open desk, protecting his papers. I'm used to this now, even glad that his distrust saves me from the tedious tax and medical forms that plague Flora. I see the thick manila envelope, labeled in my handwriting, *Driver's License*, protruding from the pigeonhole next to his bankbooks. I let my hands fall to my sides. If he is afraid to let me touch his papers, let him pull it out.

He surveys the short row of pigeonholes like a vast new territory. What first catches his eye is a packet of letters brightly edged with red and blue, air mail envelopes, accumulated letters from Italy. He looks curiously at the red and blue edge, pulls out the pile, examines his own name and address, reads the return address. "Oh, letters from Lucia." He replaces them.

I read somewhere that sight is mainly a function of memory. We see shape and color, but we identify a combination of color and density, name it, as something we have seen before. Without memory we would see as an infant does, everything new, unknown. Is that how my father sees? He sees the red and blue stripes but does not recognize the air mail design or even the shape of envelopes. Only with added clues—the shape held in his hand, the looped Italian script of his cousin, his own name, her name—can he slowly deduce what these familiar objects are.

One of my piano teachers was noted for her method of memorization, based on analysis of harmony and counterpoint, the construction of the piece. She allowed that there was also "finger memory," the body's memory of a repeated movement that should support but could never dependably replace the design held in the mind. My father must rely more and more on physical memory, finger memory. No wonder he takes such pleasure in rituals like spearing his toast or drinking coffee from a paper cup within a plastic cup with the ring through which his index finger fits just so.

He stands there as if he has even forgotten what he was looking for. (I do that all the time!) Then he reaches toward a pigeonhole and pulls out a thick, shiny gold book, my mother's address book.

I went through it after she died, looking for people who should be notified, then telling Flora, with a kind of panic in my voice, "Most of the people in here are dead!" A book of ghosts from our childhood. The distant cousin I called Nello-with-the-pretty-tie. The tough, poker-playing Asunta who kept a boarding house where my father met Tony's father when they were bachelors. A few live listings, friends like Claudette. A strange name in Delaware who turned out to have been my mother's best friend in high school. They had continued to exchange greetings at Christmas.

Last winter a friend of mine died, age forty-three, breast cancer. I looked at her name in my address book. What could I do, erase her, cross her out? Like my mother, I left the name there. In a few years I'll have a book full of dead people too. Next to my friend's name I wrote the date of her death, to guide Amy, who will probably be the one to go through my book. "Lately," she complains, "you start every sentence with, 'When I die . . . '!"

My father turns the book over in his hands a couple of times, then replaces it and pulls out a wad of newsletters from the Italian Masonic Lodge. (He last attended a meeting ten years ago, when he got a ticket for driving thirty miles an hour in the freeway speed lane.) The most recent newsletter announced the closure of that chapter, its merger with one even farther away; not enough old Italians left to support a separate group. He grunts recognition, puts them back. Beside them is a thick packet of brochures from retirement communities. Flora insisted on keeping them. He seems to know what they are, frowns, does not touch them. To the right are his bank statements, paid tax and utility bills, bank books, all the records kept in order by Flora. He reaches out toward them. She'll have another hour's work if he disarranges them.

"I think it's the brown envelope at the end, Dad. No, the next one."

He pulls out the envelope, closes the desk, looks toward the big recliner chairs in the alcove. "Shall we sit down there?"

"No." Not yet, not while I can still avoid being cornered, confined there. "It's better if we spread everything out on the table."

We sit at the end of the table, opposite his place with its setting of dishes. I pull the stack of papers out of the envelope. On top is the slim, oblong California Driver Handbook, its newsprint pages creased, ragged on the edges. There are two more copies under it, one in Vietnamese. He brought it home by mistake but won't throw it away. "Might as well be in Vietnamese," says Flora with a laugh that catches in her throat. There are other copies of the booklet scattered around the house: on top of the television set, in the magazine rack, on the table next to his bed.

"I knew I passed the written test. Here it is!"

"No, this is one you didn't pass." I pick up the long strip of newsprint and show him the red checks marking most of his answers. Beside them are other marks in blue ink, Flora's marks underlining the correct answers. She thinks he went back the next day, taking this sheet with him, copying her answers on another test, failing again. Probably they gave him a different form.

"Yeah, I missed on that one, but then I passed!"

"There's no other written test here, Dad."

"That's because she took it away from me!"

"Who took it away?"

"That woman, the same one who hit me in the eye. She pulled it right out of my hand."

"Why would she do that?"

He shrugs. Was he talking in the test area, asking someone to help him? Was that the third attempt, or the fourth?

"How many times did you take the written test?"

"I don't know, a couple of times. But I know I passed it."

"Yes, you must have passed, or you wouldn't have gone on to the driving test. But it's not here."

How did he manage to pass it? One day he produced a blank test, said it was a "sample for practice," asked me to help him do it. I read each question aloud. Before I finished reading the choice of answers, he forgot the question. I read them over and over. Finally I just checked the correct choices, connecting them up with each question, explaining over and over until he dozed off and I sat exhausted.

The next day he telephoned to announce he had passed the written test. A confabulation? No, he went on to fail the driving test. How had he passed the written test? Joe gave us his theory. "First of all, Mom, they don't give out sample tests. They gave him a test to do there. He sneaked it out, had you fill in the correct answers, sneaked it in the next day." Is that What Really Happened? Amy disagrees. "How could Grandpa plot all that out when he can't remember from one sentence to the next?'

"There it is."

"No, that's the form that says you failed the vision test."

"That woman! She hit me in the eye with that big machine so I couldn't see. Everything blurred."

The notice of failure says "This certificate signed by an eye doctor may be submitted for appeal." He nagged until Flora took him to his eye doctor, who, after a five minute exam, signed the form. Then he pushed them out of his office, refusing to listen to Flora's questions about alert vision, safe vision for driving. My father's eyes tested normal for distance, period, fifty dollars, no further questions.

What went wrong during the driver's vision test, assuming the woman didn't really hit him in the eye? Those shifting patterns of checkerboards—probably he could see them but didn't understand what he was being asked to notice.

"We have to bring the eye doctor's certificate along," I tell him. "Also the letter. Here it is. No. This is the cancellation of your license."

He drove without a license for three months. Ignoring all warnings and pleas, my father, terrified of the most petty authority, defied the law. We drove him to shopping, appointments. As soon as we had left (said his neighbors) he would ease the little pickup out of his driveway and retrace the trip to the supermarket. Finally we decided I must file the appeal for him, just to get a final, strong revocation, something that might stop him.

"There's the letter."

"No." I pick up the next sheet. "This is the one that answered the appeal," stunning me with a six-month renewal of his license, pending an appeal hearing.

"Oh, yeah," he says cheerfully. "They extended my license."

"Right," I sigh, with something like the stupefied weariness that hit me when the extension came. I stopped arguing, stopped trying to make him give it up. We would go through the process, let the officials run the show, play the whole thing out, only praying he would not hurt himself or someone else before he took his final, final test. I tried to get his brakes fixed, at least, but failed even in that. He refused to leave either car with a mechanic, no longer trusting even Flora to take his wheels out of his sight.

"Here it is." I read the letter aloud. Final appeal, final examination, written and driving. No further appeal possible except in court. He would never go to court. But will he stop driving? Flora thinks not. She talks about fulfilling his suspicions, stealing both cars. "Not stealing, perfectly legal. I'd never forgive myself if he got hurt or hurt someone else. Maybe I can get Teddy and Jennie to come up and . . ." No, I don't want to think about that yet.

"Do I have to take another written test?"

"I just read it to you, Dad. See? Written and road test."

"Oh well, you'll be with me."

"They won't let me help you, Dad."

"We'll see."

What will I do when he draws me into the test area, asks me to tell him which answers to mark?

"What's this? Oh, that joker!" At the bottom of the pile are two green sheets, nearly blank. Road tests. On one sheet a single X marks the phrase DANGEROUS MANEUVER, the pencil pressed so deeply it has torn the paper. The other has *Unsafe Vehicle* scrawled in ink across it. Both are marked FAILED above the signature of the examiner, two different signatures. "Give one of those guys a little power and he'll wreck your life!"

"No one's wrecking your life, Dad. Maybe they're trying to save it."

"What do you mean!" Not a question, a shout of outrage. "If I can't drive, I'm sunk, I'm finished!"

87

"Not at all. You don't need to drive. You only drive to the supermarket every day, and one of us is here often enough to take you there."

"I have to drive other places too."

"I wish you would, but you don't, you won't."

"I do. I have to go . . ."

"Where?" Damn it, why did I get into this old script?

"To . . . the bank!" he says righteously and, full of triumph, remembers, "To the doctor!"

"Flora takes you to the bank, and I take you to the doctor. You refuse to go to the senior center anymore. Where else is there?"

He is not looking at me now, but his hands are fists, ready to lunge, punch. At me?

"Look, Dad, I hope you will get out more, but if you do, you can take a cab. Did you look at the car insurance bill before Flora paid it?" I know she made him examine it, hoping to appeal to his frugality. "Just with what you pay in car insurance, you could take a cab two or three times a week. Then there's gas and . . ."

"So you think I'll have to take another written test." His knuckles are white, his head bowed as if ready to butt any wall, no matter how hard and thick.

"That's what the letter says."

He reaches out, takes one of the handbooks. "Then let's go over this book again." He opens it, frowns. "Where are my glasses?" They are, as always, on the stack of unread newspapers beside his recliner chair in the TV alcove.

I know just what he will say now.

"Why don't you just read some of this stuff to me? Let's sit over there and be comfortable." He gets up. We will sit in the recliners. I will begin to read. After five minutes, he will doze off. Well, better that than more arguments. I get up.

I hear chimes, three descending notes, a sound I hardly ever hear in this house: the front doorbell. "Expecting someone?"

He shakes his head.

"Want me to get it?"

"No, no," he says anxiously, hurrying across the room to open the door beside the refrigerator. As he walks through the doorway into the dim front rooms, he half-closes the door, as if to block my view of the front door. Now I am quite sure I know who it is.

He opens the front door a few inches, letting in sunlight and a harsh giggling voice. His face is lit in an uneasy smile. He nods, inching backward as the door is pushed open, and the slightly guttural voice says, "Aren't you going to let me in, Petey?"

My father was baptized Pietro. All his life he has been called Pete, never Petey.

She pushes past him. "Don't have much time, gave up my lunch hour to get them." With the sun behind her, I see only a short, shadowy figure carrying a large box. She moves quickly, surely, a woman who knows her way around this house. She enters the kitchen with a sudden surge, gasping as she lunges toward the kitchen table and drops a box of apricots on it.

I look at her curiously, and she sizes me up. Throughout this year of hints, then rumors, then phone calls, then Flora's alarms and ultimatums, I wondered, what does she look like? At all like my mother? Not at all.

She is a little older than I but still in her fifties. Short, plump, tottering on high heels made of cheap, scuffed plastic. A run in her stocking crosses her thick ankle. Her faded polyester dress hikes up a little over her backside, and the buttoned front strains, opening gaps between buttons, revealing a dingy bra. What a strange sight in this kitchen. The word that comes to mind is . . . slatternly. Couldn't she at least have had a dash of disreputable style?

Her face is pale, pasty, with some irregularity around the upper lip—an old scar? Her eyes are pale too; she blinks frequently, avidly, taking me in. She timed this visit so that finally we would meet. She knew when I would be coming and why. "You're Pat, aren't you, the teacher with the lovely singing voice." She asserts her knowledge, her power. She knows so much more about me than I know about her. "I am Develia."

I nod. "You're kidding," laughed my neighbor when I told him the name of "that woman" as my father always calls her. "Develia, devil, Delilah, the temptress. You're making this up!" No. I only wish I were. I picked up her name from her business card, always lying near the phone. The card also revealed that she works in one of the offices of the county bureaucracy. Her exalted title denotes a mid-level clerical job, Joe says.

My father has closed the front door and followed her into the kitchen. He stands behind her, eyeing me nervously.

"I finally found some nice ones, Petey. Petey's been calling and calling me to get him some apricots because his didn't do so well this year, and I know this farmer who's got a bit of orchard left just behind that computer plant, near the school?" Her guttural accent (German?) sounds less heavy than it does on the phone.

I look toward my father, but he says nothing. Both of them are waiting for me, both beginning to look more relaxed. The moment for me to make an angry or rude denunciation has already passed. Develia has judged that the younger daughter, Pat, is a lesser obstacle than the alert, determined Flora. That is why she planned this encounter. If there is a weak point in the wall of resistance, it must be Pat.

"I can't stay long. Have to get back to the office. No rest for the wicked, eh, Petey?" She laughs more easily, loudly, and as my father lets himself smile back at her, she winks and smirks at all the ironies of her joke—that she is the "wicked" woman Petey wants to move into his house despite his daughters' opposition. I almost admire her defiance. I won't tell Flora that.

"You owe me ten dollars, Petey."

"Huh?" My father goes vague, as usual when asked for money.

"Ten dollars, Petey." She giggles. "They cost me ten dollars, a bargain, but I'm not a rich woman, can't afford to give them away!" How well she handles his tightness—brashly, directly, good humoredly. This time she winks at me, sharing the joke of his penny-pinching. She knows how unnecessary it is, knows his worth down to the last penny, knew it before we knew she existed. "And my feet are killing me!"

I nod toward a chair, and she sits down, eyeing the papers on the table while my father takes out his wallet, looks into it, shakes his head, and says, "Just a minute." He goes through the hall door toward his bedroom, where he keeps cash in a can on the closet shelf.

I'm sure Develia knows about that can, too. During one of her first visits, when my father dozed off in his recliner, did she go through the desk, through the whole house, and decide the stakes were high enough? Or did she learn he had money and then seek him out? Does she follow obituaries and search county tax records? We make wild guesses because we have never learned exactly how they met. We thought "that woman" referred to a neighbor who used to visit my mother. By the time we knew "that woman" was someone named Develia, he was insisting that she move in. "But who is she? Where did you meet her?" He could not remember. When Flora telephoned her, she claimed to have once lived nearby and known my mother, but neighbors claimed ignorance of any Develia.

"So, he's going to try again," she says, looking at the papers on the table and shaking her head. No giggles and winks now. She looks intently into my eyes, all serious concern. "He shouldn't drive. He hardly knows where he's going, never looks. Did he tell you he got lost driving back from the supermarket on Tuesday? Came out a different side of the parking lot and went round and round until he almost ran out of gas before he figured out how to get home."

I shake my head. She nods with satisfaction, having established that my father confides in her what he hides from me.

"He told me if they deny his appeal, he's going to drive anyway!"

"I wouldn't be surprised."

"You know what that means? His insurance company will cancel him. If he hits someone, they'll sue, and he'll lose everything, the house, the lot, every cent he has in the bank!"

Indeed, she does know each item of his worth.

"Even if they just catch him driving without a license. I talked to a friend on the police force, and he says they have to arrest him, put him in jail."

A threat, now? Empty, I think.

"An old man like that, it would kill him!"

Oh, Develia, you're overplaying it. You disappoint me,

thinking that's the way to scare me into agreeing he needs you. Funny how some people (me) mistake silence for wisdom and how others (her) mistake it for stupidity.

"But when there's someone here with him, he doesn't insist on driving. He lets someone drive him around."

Someone. Guess who.

"And it's not only the driving. Remember the time I called you when I found him here asleep in the chair, no dinner, a pot of canned soup burning on the stove? He pretends to be doing all right alone here, but he calls me ten times a day because he can't . . ."

"No, he doesn't pretend to be doing well," I interrupt. "He calls us ten times a day too, but he makes it very hard for us to help him."

"Well, you're so far away. I'm right here. And he wants me. You know, when Flora made him call me and tell me not to come back, he phoned me as soon as she left, as if nothing had happened."

That scene must have been high melodrama, never before played in this kitchen. I'm almost sorry I missed it. At the time I was glad to be in bed with the flu while Flora screamed at him, "I won't have that woman in my mother's house, touching my mother's things," and, yes, ending with "over my dead body!" That scene cost Flora. Three days later she was hospitalized with gastroenteritis, a price she paid willingly, she said, for a final showdown. She was mistaken. Every week brought a final showdown, a final capitulation by my father, instantly forgotten by him.

"Old people love me. It's because I understand them, how to make them happy. I'd work just taking care of old people if I could afford to, but I have to keep my job." Her pale, avid eyes are beamed at me so intensely that I want to say, turn down the lights, the volume. "Petey just needs someone here for dinner and the night, and that would be just right for both of us. He's so sweet, and we get along so well. I cheer him, I know how to . . ."

I wait for her to pause so that I can tell her we have decided to withdraw our opposition, but she goes on and on, talking faster and faster as if she is afraid to let me speak.

"Now," she takes a breath, lowers her voice a bit, smiles. "You could talk to your sister. I think you want your father to have what he wants. You're more broadminded."

What does that mean? Probably he has referred to me as his divorced daughter from the wicked city.

"I know I said something you didn't like, but I'm sure you misunderstood. Petey told me you got pretty upset, but he couldn't remember what he told you I said. I'm sure we can clear that up so we understand each other."

I'm annoyed that he passed on to her what I said. What was it? Oh, yes, she phoned me and said he'd told her his family cared for nothing but his money. For a minute I was furious at him, him and his damned money! But when I hung up I thought, wait. That didn't ring true, not the kind of thing he would say, even to us, let alone to someone outside the family. Could it be something she invented, to offend us, start a quarrel, drive us away, abandoning him to her? I telephoned him and asked if he had ever said such a thing. "No, never. She's a liar, not the kind of woman I want in my house." Ten minutes later he called back cheerfully telling me he'd found "this woman" who wanted to move in.

"It was only a joke. One night he said his daughters didn't like me, so I said to him, well, Petey, I guess we'll just have to elope to Reno and get married."

Out of her own mouth. No, he never told anyone about that.

"He just laughed. We both laughed and laughed. It was just a joke."

How many times has she tried to bundle him off to Reno? A risky tactic, a serious miscalculation if it fails. She must have thought he had told us. No wonder she's nervous. So, he wouldn't go. All he wants is a free caretaker. Is each of them conning the other? Maybe they deserve each other.

"We have so many jokes together. I know how to make him laugh. It's good for him to laugh."

He comes back into the room, holding out a ten dollar bill. I inject a question into the silence. "How is your son?" One of the few facts we know about her, one that makes her more human, is that she has a crippled son who lives with her.

"Just fine," she says brightly. Her tone reminds me a little of mine when people ask me how Joe is. "Aren't these good apricots, Petey?"

"I understand he just graduated from college."

"That's right. Now, Petey, if you need help freezing these . . ."

"And he's found a job in the city?"

"No, he'll stay home with me for a while. He needs to be near the doctor here for his treatments."

"Then I misunderstood. Dad, I thought you said Develia's son was moving to the city."

"No, I can handle it myself," he says, looking at the apricots, ignoring my question.

Develia's smiling mask has slipped a little. She looks irritated. My father keeps looking at the apricots, avoiding eye contact with either of us. Develia means to keep her son with her, bring him here. My father staunchly confabulates the son moving to the city. How will they resolve it? Who will give in? She's tough, but in his mild, quiet way my father has never given in to anyone. My mother denied him his own way only once: she died.

"Well, I have to get back to work. Bye, bye, Pat." She goes through the door to the front rooms. Her wobble on her high heels looks weary, stiff; her feet hurt her, as mine do now after a run. (My older friends say it's time to switch to swimming.) Like me, Develia is single, with a civil service job that doesn't pay much. Her son has problems, needs, an illness with no cure. Like mine. Maybe she is nothing worse than an aging woman trying to survive, ease her burdens, get free housing, a resourceful way to increase the money for her son's special needs. And I am a snob who despises a woman who wears plastic shoes.

My father follows her with some lightness in his step. His face is animated as it was at the barber shop. He needs people like her, people he cannot lean on, dead weight, as he leans on his daughters. He needs people who shake him out of himself.

Suddenly I am shaken out of my rationalizing. In the shadows near the front door, I see her reach out to nudge him, below the belt, murmuring some giggling, guttural sound, a come-on, a line from an old Marlene Dietrich movie scene acted by a female impersonator. He jumps back. His recoil is unmistakable, a panicky, not-in-front-of-my-daughter reflex. She laughs and leans to hiss something at him, and he smiles. Did she mean me to see it, the sexual touch between them? If so, she has fumbled, overplayed again, displaying her tawdry titillation, her bad imitation of desire. Does he buy it? Yes, he was afraid to let me see—guilty, priggish, but pleased, flattered. No fool like an old fool.

"Come on out, Petey, walk me to my car." They open the front door and walk out through the shaft of sunlight. Will she kiss him goodbye for the benefit of the neighbors?

I am living in a soap opera. No, a soap opera siren would be more attractive, more credible. I can't believe in this one.

I never believed in her, certainly not when I first mentioned her to Doctor Rayman. He had almost pushed me out the door, as usual, without a word or a glance, when I remembered Flora's insistence that I tell him, "There's some woman named Develia, doesn't seem to connect with old friends or neighbors. He wants her to move in, and my sister wonders if . . ." Doctor Rayman actually jumped, actually forgot himself enough to look into my face. "Get his bankbooks out of the house," he shouted. "Get a lawyer, tell him to call me. Now. I'll certify him. Conservatorship. Don't waste a minute. These people come out of the woodwork whenever someone dies. By the time you know what's happening, it's too late, the money's gone and . . . get a lawyer! Isn't your daughter . . . ?"

Yes. Amy sent us to a friend who specializes in estate law. He said an Irrevocable Trust would be simpler than conservatorship, "if your father will sign it. I'll draw it up. Bring him in." Up to the last moment I doubted he would sign, but Flora had no doubts. "If I tell him it's all right, another tax form or something, he'll sign. I'm always giving him things to sign." The good daughter. The trusted daughter. He barely glanced at the first page before he signed. Does he know he spends each penny only by our permission, needs our signatures for any business? If so, he pretends he keeps complete control, and so do we.

We thought of telling Develia about the Trust, or leaving copies of it around for her to see, the best test of her real intentions. Maybe she would read it and disappear. Amy advised silence. "Best to have the Trust in place, unchallenged, as long as possible. In case she tries to put doubts in Grandpa's head." Unchallenged? How irrevocable is irrevocable? "And remember, if she does move in, does keep house for him, she'll probably claim something when he dies, and you'll have to work out some fair recompense for her time."

So it was decided that today, after he loses, once and for

all, his place in the driver's seat, I will tell him that we no longer oppose Develia's moving in. I have rehearsed my new line. "It's your decision, Dad." He is legally protected, so we must respect his right to choose how he wants to live. And with whom.

Yet, now that I have finally seen her, seen her avid eyes . . . . if she moves in, caters to him, flatters him, bows to his stubborn will, then somehow learns about the Trust, what might she do? We read these stories in the newspapers—old people threatened, abused, even killed. The culprits always look so ordinary. They abuse and terrorize some ordinary person in some ordinary house. Why not this house?

The front door closes. I watch him walk through the dim front rooms carrying papers in his hands. He steps into the kitchen, carefully closes the door, and comes to the table.

"Oh, your mail came. Let me clear this up first." I put the letter confirming his appointment and the certificate from his eye doctor into my purse, then gather up the other booklets and paper, stuff them into the manila envelope, return it to the desk.

"Where are my glasses?"

I point to the stand next to his recliner. He gets them, sits down at the table with me, takes the glasses out of the case and puts them on, slowly, ceremoniously. He picks up each envelope, studies it, then puts it down again, frowns, shrugs.

"Looks like mostly junk mail, Dad."

He grunts and pushes the envelopes toward me. I sort them into two piles, putting the first class envelopes in front of him, with the airmail-striped one on top. "Looks like a letter from Italy, Dad." I pick up the advertising to throw it into the wastebasket.

"Wait! Now just wait a minute."

My mother always sorted the mail, answered it with letters or checks, read him what he needed to know. Flora does the same. I am allowed to sort his mail, but then he examines my decisions and categories. I put the stack of bulk mail in front of him.

He takes out his pocket knife and slits open a thick envelope. Out fall sheets of colorful stamps, certificates with gold seals, a letter printed in three colors. "What's all this?"

"It says you may have won a million," I laugh. "All you have to do to find out is subscribe to all these magazines."

He snorts and pushes the papers from him. The next envelope, not so flashy, contains a single sheet of paper with a return envelope. He scans the letter impatiently, uncomprehendingly, then pushes it toward me.

"Want to contribute fifty dollars to the Republican Party?"

He does not bother to answer. He has voted Republican all his life, but any political act beyond voting—a letter or a contribution—he would consider an act of fanaticism.

We examine, identify, and reject a sale at the hardware store, an offer of life insurance, and an invitation to tour "choice property" in northeastern Oregon. Now he allows me to dump the junk mail into the waste basket. "This too."

I glance at the envelope he hands me. "I don't think so. This looks like your phone bill."

He snatches it from my hand, reads the return address, then gets up. "Don't lose that! Don't fool with it! Let Flora to take care of it!" He carries it to the desk, squeezes it into a little spiral rack on top. His voice and manner imitate Flora's desperate pleadings against his sabotage of her work. Second or third notices arrive for bills he has lost and insists he already paid. He complains that he has not received his Social Security check; after phone calls, letters, Flora learns that he cashed the check and put the money in the can on the shelf in his bedroom. Flora has changed his billing address; soon all bills and checks will go directly to her.

He puts aside the airmail-striped envelope and picks up one from Modern Properties. "Read it to me?"

"'Confirming our conversation last week . . .'" Did that real estate woman come here to the house?"

He nods happily. "She can get me thirty thousand for the lot!" he announces, confident that I will be impressed.

I mumble my lines half-heartedly. "Worth three times . . ."

"Got to sell that lot. Can't take care of it . . . those taxes . . ."

I pick up the next envelope and feel a tightening around my stomach as I see the return address. Fernwood Cemetery. What now?

A week after the funeral I took my father, and more flowers, to the cemetery. I meant to comfort him, please him. He surprised me with his sullen aversion to the place, his refusal to stand by while I arranged the flowers, his refusal to look at the catalog of headstones. Each week, when I came to him, I offered to drive him to the cemetery. No. What he really wanted me to do, he said, was to enlarge and frame a recent photograph of my mother, taken at his eightieth birthday party, just before she died. "Sure, Dad, no problem."

As soon as the photograph was on the wall he told me to have her body exhumed and cremated, then sell the two burial plots. I delayed. I thought, when he finds out that he will not make any money on the plots, he will forget about it. He did not. Week after week, he nagged until I arranged the cremation, simple enough, a phone call, a check he reluctantly signed.

I rip open the envelope.

"What's that?"

"From the cemetery people."

"Oh, the refund."

"No, Dad." Wearily, I go back to that old script. "There won't be any refund."

"But those plots are worth plenty! We had them twenty years. People pay ten time what we paid to get plots in that cemetery!"

"Probably. But the cemetery would only give you back what you paid for them. It cost that much to exhume the body. Another four hundred for a wooden casket, because Mom was buried in a metal casket, and that won't burn. Or so they said. Then another four hundred for the cremation."

"We could have sold those plots and made enough to pay for all that and more."

"Maybe. But I would have had to advertise them in the paper, take people to see them, negotiate price and title, and . . . Dad, I just don't have time for all that, and neither does Flora."

"Bunch of crooks!"

I nod. The letter supports his accusation. Fernwood Cemetery now wants another hundred, a "transfer charge." I fold the letter, stuff it into my purse.

"What is it? What?"

"Nothing. They want more money. Don't worry, they won't get a penny. I'll see to it. Forget it." In my mind I am already composing a letter to them—righteous, blistering, threatening. I let my anger rise, my displaced anger, anger at my father for what he did, what I helped him do to my mother's body.

"How do I even know that little box—that those ashes are really . . ."

"You don't. Did Flora take them yet?"

He shakes his head.

"I thought you wanted her to scatter them at sea."

He nods. "I'm going to give them to her next time she comes."

Flora refuses to take the box of ashes until he hands them to her calmly, without moaning and trembling. They go through a weekly ritual, she taking the box of ashes to her car, he following, moaning, she stopping, turning back, returning the box to the drawer of my mother's vanity (well hidden under clothing so that Rosetta, who is superstitious, will not know the ashes are in the house). "Not until you're ready to give them up, Dad," says Flora, denying him resolution of the drama she says he has invented to cover and excuse his real act. This is a small punishment she deals out to him for what he did. She is still angry, but unlike me, feels no guilt. "It was his right, his choice, his stubborn obsession. If you had refused to arrange it, I'd have had to, and I'm too busy with all this tax stuff."

"I couldn't drive down there," he says, as if accused. "I don't even know where the cemetery is."

I do. A ten minute drive. I offered to take him there every week. It would have given us something to do.

"I couldn't even find her grave."

Because he wouldn't order a headstone.

"Why leave her there? Among strangers."

Stranger than the Pacific Ocean?

"Better to have something here to remind me of her. That picture you took of her at my birthday party."

Hanging beside your chair in the television alcove, that place where she lay helplessly listening to your rambling repetitions. Yes, you've put her back in that corner with you, denied her a resting place anywhere else.

"So they sent a check for the difference. Better give it to Flora."

"There's no difference. It cost you the two plots, plus eight hundred dollars to have the body exhumed and cremated."

102

It used to give me a grim satisfaction to tell him what his money-making scheme had cost him. Until the day Flora quietly told me the conclusion she had reached. "It wasn't the money. It was revenge."

Now and then my mother would remind me that these burial plots were paid for, ready. A casual reminder, and my indifferent "Sure, Mom, I won't forget." Maybe her feelings ran deeper than she showed. Maybe she bought the burial plots so long ago because she had heard me voice my "modern" preference for cremation. Maybe she hated the idea and wanted to make sure it would not be done to her body. If that was her feeling, my father must have known how deep it lay. Maybe he opposed spending the money for cemetery plots even then, and she took one of her rare opposing stands against his will; that was why she had appealed to us to carry out her wishes. Flora said, "It was revenge, spite. He was getting back at her for dying on him, leaving him." Was I my father's accomplice in an act that seems more twisted and ugly as time passes? Is that What Really Happened?

"Ah, a letter from Lucia." He has saved for the last his letter from Italy. "Want to try it?"

"Sure."

He acknowledges that my schoolbook Italian is nearly as good as his (less familiar to him than the unwritten dialect spoken by his parents). I have even taken up the correspondence that was my mother's duty, the thin thread of contact maintained for two generations with cousins who existed, for Flora and me, only in letters and snapshots. When my parents visited their cousins twenty-five years ago, they were convinced that their trip would be the last reunion of a family divided not only by an ocean but by the indifference of their daughters toward such distant ties.

Five years ago I surprised them and myself by impulsively grabbing a bargain flight to Rome. I would zig-zag, train by train, town by town, for a month, north to the village of their birth. They seemed both pleased and uneasy, reminding me that, "The family there is very traditional." Clearly they did not see their divorced daughter as their chosen delegate to the old country.

I didn't know what to expect—not what I found. The factory village my grandparents had left is now a quiet suburb of Turin, a stop on the way to ski resorts in the Alps. My cousins, whatever they may have thought, welcomed me handsomely. These were my people, without doubt: prudent, hard-working, dutiful to family, conservative. They were pleased that I was musical—it runs in the family, of course— and interested in my teaching people from so many different countries. They too were living with the dislocations of our times, including the inrush of poorer, darker immigrants. They worried about the same changes, saw the same television, suffered family tensions and conflicts. Like their American cousins, they had prospered. They had built spacious houses beyond the ruined medieval village (now being restored, cherished, embellished—no more dirt floors). Their children attended university, displayed their fluent English, their bright prospects, their plans to visit America, as tourists, of course. The town and they were not what my parents had left behind, not even what they had visited twenty years before.

Throughout my return flight, I wondered if my *nonna* had been right to resist, to delay following her husband to America. What, after all, had been the point of crossing an ocean and a continent through prejudice and poverty, fear and anger, killing work and bitter sacrifice? Wouldn't it have been better to stay in Italy and see it through to better times?

A statistic Joe found in a history book set me straight. During the thirty years culminating in my grandparents' emigration, Italy exported one-third of its people. We took *la miseria* with us, made space, made it possible for the rest of the family to cohere, to survive, and even, eventually, to prosper.

I take the tissue-thin page from my father and begin to read. *"Ho ricevuto la tua lettera . . ."*

I stop, amazed. During the sixteen months since my mother died, he has talked about writing to his cousin. He would write, he had written, he would write again—a phantom correspondence confabulated each time a note or greeting card arrived. I have never seen him write a letter in either English or Italian, correspondence being the women's work of our family. How could he now, impaired as he is? Yet somehow he finally accomplished the miracle, wrote a letter in a language he hardly remembers, addressed it, stamped it with sufficient postage, sent it off. The proof is here. Lucia has received it.

"Quest'estate siamo tutti contenti perché . . . what's this word?"

We huddle over the loops which resemble no alphabet. Together we deduce a reference to *le mie nipoti*, her granddaughters, wonderful, spirited girls who showed me around Turin. When they learned I had read Cesare Pavese, they took me to Caffé Elena, where he used to sip espresso. There we sat in a dark corner and pretended it was the corner where he sat dreaming up his sad stories. I miss those girls. I miss old Lucia, who was constantly slipping back into dialect, which, after a few hours, I found I could understand better than Italian, the voice of my *nonna* imprinted in my brain. I'd like to go back again.

"I'd like to go back again," my father repeats my thought. Is Amy right? Does his dementia give him some power to invade my mind?

"What?"

"Back to Italy. You and Flora could come with me."

"Uh . . . I don't think I could afford it right now, Dad."

"I'll pay for everything. How's that sound?"

Like a nightmare. My mind races through the strenuous process of travel. Hard enough without him, his fears and obsessions, his crushing will, his abject weakness. His terror of the unfamiliar, disguised as contempt. His penny-pinching. I can't persuade him to go across town; now he wants to go across the world.

"School starts next week. I'm committed till next summer."

"You're off at Christmas. We could go for two weeks. I just want to see the old town, visit my cousins before we old ones all die." To sit in *their* kitchens asking the same questions over and over again. Or carping. My mother told me she was ashamed when they took that trip because all he did was criticize, tell everyone how much better we did things in America.

"It'll be cold. They get snow up there. I don't know if you're up to it. We could ask your doctor." Now why did I say that? Doctor Rayman will probably say the trip will do him good, stimulate him. My father would be shaken out of his depression. With the two of us to care for him, he would be fine. Twenty-four hours a day. Yes, he'll be fine. Flora and I will collapse.

"I'll tell Flora when she comes, surprise her," he says, almost cheerfully. "If I'm going to go, better go soon."

Will this become the new obsession, something to replace his driver's license, the subject of ten phone calls a day? And so reasonable, desirable, adventurous. Why deny a lonely old man who wants to take us to Europe? Maybe he'll change his mind when he sees the cost of air fare. No, it'll be like the cremation—what he wants, he'll pay for.

Anxiety, anger, shame, rise in a crowd of scrambled, crazy thoughts, ungenerous, mean thoughts. Why couldn't he have died first? Then Flora and I would have taken our mother on a trip. How gladly I would wheelchair my mother all over Europe! She would have been someone else without him. We three women would have laughed and cried together, discovered each other. We would have spoken the truth to each other for once.

"No, it's better that she died first."

He does pick up frayed edges of my thoughts!

"What would she have done without me?"

What indeed.

"She couldn't even drive!" He sighs. "What time is it?"

"A little after two."

"What time is my test?"

"Four."

"What do you say we watch a little television?"

"Okay." It can't be put off any longer.

The two brown recliner chairs face a big console television. Smaller pieces crowd the floor from the television to the recliners: a coffee table holding a neat stack of *Reader's Digest* magazines; an unused record player; a rack holding a dozen records, Lawrence Welk and Pavarotti; two metal folding trays, one covered by a stack of newspapers. "What would you like to watch?"

"Whatever you want, Dad." His schedule of shows is as fixed as his taste in food. If I choose something else he will fidget, sigh, mumble, and eventually ask, "Mind if I change it?" to a familiar talk or game show. Then he will settle down, content, and doze off, waking only if I change the channel.

He studies the front page of the top newspaper, nods,

murmurs, "Friday." The neat stack of newspapers is un-opened, untouched. I think he no longer reads anything but the date across the top, several times a day, to place himself in time. He puts the newspaper down, picks up *TV Guide.* "What time is it?"

"Two-twenty."

He nods again, turns pages, nods, then turns on the television and sets the channel. The screen flashes a black-and-white picture. Turning a couple of dials will bring back the color, but we have given up adjusting the set; as soon as we leave, he dials away the color. Why? Does it hurt his eyes? He evades our questions, and we stop asking, stop adjusting. "At least," Flora laughs, "it's not like when he was playing with the dials in the refrigerator—no frozen milk and liquid ice cream."

The television erupts with a game show, wheels spinning, lights flashing, bells ringing, audience cheering.

He sits down in his chair, near the desk, near the wall where the last photograph taken of my mother hangs. I sit in her chair. We set our hands firmly on the armrests, then give a straight-armed push. Our chairs tilt backward, and a platform rises to elevate our legs. I feel like a beetle on its back, immobilized, trapped, vulnerable. The vinyl is cold and slippery; in a few minutes it will warm to my body heat and stick to my skin. Is this how she felt during those long afternoons and long evenings while the television cackled and my father snored or, worse, talked? Those eternal evenings after she stopped complaining.

"I miss your mother so much."

"So do I." I never thought I would. I thought both she and I would be free when she died.

"It's not the same!" he snaps resentfully. "Fifty-five years!"

"I know, Dad. I only meant . . ."

"Nobody knows what it's like. The loneliness. It's the loneliness that kills you. If I just had someone here, a woman to cook a little. She could have her own room, rent free." He pauses, waits, and when I say nothing, dares to go on. "There's . . . this woman. She's a pretty good cook. She'd like to live closer to her job. She's . . . that woman . . . you know . . ."

"Develia."

"That's right. You don't like her?"

I shrug, then shake my head, no.

"But I need someone! If I . . . that woman could stay here . . ."

"It's your decision, Dad." There. It's done.

Silence. I have snapped the tape of our old argument, thrown away the script, put in a new line. He tries to pick up a familiar line somewhere, throw me a cue. "I'm not looking for someone to sleep with me. She'd have her own room, do a little cooking. What's wrong with that?"

"It's your decision, Dad. Do what you want. I won't butt in anymore. Okay? Let's just forget it and watch TV."

We watch a young black woman who frowns deeply, says a word hopefully, then leaps up, waving her arms. The audience cheers. The music rises. She has guessed something correctly. She is happy. Everyone is happy.

"Flora doesn't like her."

"That's right."

"Flora won't let her move in."

"She will if that's what you want."

He turns to look at me with his usual doubts about my judgment.

"Do you want to call Flora and ask her? She's changed her mind, decided not to oppose Develia if you want her to move in. You can do what you want."

"You sure?"

"Call Flora."

He raises his head, then lets it fall back again. "Later," he sighs, "after this program."

"Okay."

"I miss her so much." He turns his head away from me, toward the photograph on the wall beside his chair. "We had everything so perfect, finally, after all those hard years. We had everything . . . and then . . . why . . . ?"

"She was sick a long time," I mumble my line, refusing to follow his gaze up to that sad photograph.

"But she was always delicate, nervous. She never got a good start. That father of hers."

I nod.

"When he was born, his mother threw him out in the bushes."

"Mom's father? Really!" A new bit of family history uncovered. This has the ring of truth. Not a confabulation, a memory buried deep because it is so terrible.

"Yep. Then someone went out, and he was still alive, so they brought him back in." He shakes his head. "What kind of people would do a thing like that?"

Who can tell? When I visited the village, I found only one cousin on my mother's side, a shy, pious, pale spinster, a ghost of a woman, who spent all her time in charity work for her church. The rest of that family had scattered, disappeared.

"So I guess he had it bad too, but why take it out on her? Believe me, if it hadn't been for me, the way I took care of her, she wouldn't have lived as long as she did."

He waits a few seconds, then accepts my silence as confirmation.

"Yeah, she did pretty good up until your divorce, but that

110

finished her." He shakes his head as if I struck the fatal blow last year instead of twenty years ago.

The first time my father said this aloud, after one of my mother's heart attacks, I felt almost relieved to hear it finally spoken, the accusation I had heard in unanswerable silence for years. Not that I tried to answer it. What could I say, that I had never caused my mother pain and worry?

"I hear Tony became an alcoholic."

Here comes the sequel to the saga of Pat, the Mother Killer. Tony was seen drunk or hung over several times during the two years before he remarried.

"Is he still alive?"

"Of course, he's alive," I snap, more sharply than I meant to. I shrug, loosen up. "He married a rich woman, moved to Palm Springs, had another family, lives very well." I laugh. I've always thought this a good joke on all the people—including me—who said or thought "poor Tony." My father gives me a sidelong glance of reproving disbelief. "Amy was just down there for a weekend. She told you all about it. Don't you remember?"

No. Such a story does not fit in with What Really Happened as he confabulated it long before his mind began to fail.

"We always thought that you . . . so smart and talented and pretty when you were young . . . that you'd be the one to make a good life." He makes a motion with his hands, a sign of collapse, of shame from which he turns away his eyes.

"Dad, I have made a good life." My voice has tightened to a croak, probably because I'm trying not to scream. "I have a fine son and daughter. I have a job I love, work I'm proud to do. Good friends. Good health." I almost add the ultimate defense—there were even a couple of men who wanted to marry me. Would that redeem me in his eyes? Not likely.

Besides, he has already forgotten what he said; he is watching a near-naked blonde spin a wheel on the television screen.

Why am I defending myself? In a few hours I will go back to my real life, which needs no defense. But here in this kitchen I am sucked into a hell inhabited by Kafka and my mother, filled with her fear of blame and shame, fault and failure. Whether it was a dirt spot on the floor or a daughter's divorce, it was her disgrace. "What did I do to deserve this?" was a genuine question. She could not believe in misfortune, only in retribution, punishment. More beatings from an angry God who looked like her father? An unlikely shadow over a family that never went to church.

Here in her chair I regress to those pre-dawn hours of twenty years ago, when I would lie awake, accuser, judge and jury at my unending trial, the verdict known before I even committed the crime. Guilty of destroying my children's home, guilty of exiling their innocent father, guilty of breaking my mother's heart. Why rebel now? I would ask myself at four in the morning. Why, after a dozen years with a loving, faithful man who puts up with all my crazy moods? What about our children, his family, my family? I would lie awake and count the people—never fewer than forty—who would be hurt if I could not put down this crazy rebellion exploding in me.

It was Flora who gave an answer of sorts to my questions. When rumors of trouble in my marriage began to seep silently, like an unmentionable stain, through the family, she took me aside at one of our family dinners. "I know exactly what you are going through," she said. "No one knows better than I do how you feel."

I leaned toward her like an exhausted, drowning swimmer, reaching for this buoy of acknowledgement, this simple YES. Then I wasn't crazy? There was something real I was fighting? Someone who understood, someone I could talk to? She put her arms around me and whispered into my ear with gentle finality, "And you will have to learn to resign yourself." I stiffened, backed away, a silent NO! streaking up my backbone. At that moment we were called to help serve dinner.

Within a week I had managed to "destroy my family," as Tony moaned when he moved back to his mother's house to stay until he remarried.

Not until several years after I made the break did I begin to understand the instinct that drove me. Then I could look back on that crucial Christmas dinner, that Norman Rockwell scene, one of many warm, sprawling family scenes Amy and Joe recall so fondly. Then I could discern the pattern taken for granted, unnoticed by the children who laughed and quarreled and watched their mothers passing the richly-laden platters among the men who had wooed and won them. Men who drank a little too much, or idled between jobs a little too long, or puttered absent-mindedly in a business kept afloat by a wife, or owed a little too much for another new car, or teased the women and children with jokes that were a little too cruel. Easy going men, untroubled by any event or thought that did not threaten their own comfort. Blind to any problem until after their wives had solved it. Heedless of the set mouths and flashing eyes of these anxious, difficult women, whose worst misfortune or disgrace would be to lose these men, to fail this relation.

Even more years passed before I realized how fragile this family picture was, actually, how vital that I "learn to resign" myself. One piece plucked from the scene cracked the image. Other cracks followed: dissension, relocation, death, divorce—no stranger to the next generation. Only scattered bits and pieces remain.

Flora and I have never spoken of that day. Probably she has forgotten it. I can hardly remember the unhappy young women we were twenty years ago. No doubt each of us found the solution she could live with. Or . . . maybe there are no solutions, only choices that, at the time, make life possible. Then we change, times change, old structures collapse, old patterns dissolve, new problems arise. Maybe that's What Really Happens. Now we are two graying women with a new problem that has no solution. We draw closer together to share its weight, encourage and relieve one another, commiserate, agreeing that part of coping with it is learning to resign ourselves.

A red-haired girl is whooping and squealing at the refrigerator she has won. I glance at my father to see if the show amuses him. His eyes are shut, his mouth open. He is asleep.

I look up at the wall beside me where high school graduation photos of grandchildren surround a formal portrait of my parents. Flora's Jennie, Beth and Teddy are on the right, my Amy and Joe on the left. There was a brief time, Flora told me, when Joe's photo was taken down. By the time I arrived a few days later to talk to my parents, to "explain," the photo was back up on the wall, although my mother was still vomiting, my father muttering the inevitable, "Better to hear he was dead."

Yet where did my own enlightened friends stand then, not so many years ago, even in the wicked city? I remember the party where they joked about our standing squeezed between generations. "How do you tell your parents that your son is getting divorced?" Laughter. "That's nothing. How do you tell your parents your daughter is living with a man?" Laughter. "That's nothing. How do you tell your parents she's pregnant and doesn't want to marry him?" Weaker laughter. Then I topped them all. "How do you tell your

114

parents your son is gay?' No one laughed. One of them silently handed me a slip of paper on which he had written the name of "a therapist who's good at these neuroses traceable to the mother." (He now insists he can't remember ever doing such a silly thing.)

In the end, I answered my own question in a cowardly, cruel way. When Joe phoned from college to say his coming-out gesture would be a signed letter printed in the next issue of *Time* (an act of courage unheard of then), I knew the day had come when I must tell them, must forewarn them, must be the buffer, take the anger, accusations, weeping, collapse. It would be the drama of my divorce all over again, only worse.

I ducked it, telling Joe he should forewarn them. He wrote them a letter of curt bravado, just what one would expect of a terrified twenty-year-old. But it wouldn't have mattered what he wrote. I had ducked nothing. Summoned by one of my father's then rare phone calls, made only when my mother was ill, I went to take added blame: how could I not have prepared them for such a blow? Only Amy could salvage a smile, one good thing in that mess. With her cousins in a dropout phase—from a marriage, a job, a school—and her little brother in disgrace, "It's kind of fun to be the one good grandchild for a while."

I will take a lesson from Amy and that old, awful scene. I find one good thing about the death of my mother. I will never have to prepare her for AIDS.

The large photo in the center was taken just after my parents retired. My mother, not many years older than I am now, is seated, my father perched on the arm of her chair, leaning toward her, one hand touching her arm. Both of them are formally dressed and posed, looking directly into the camera, their mouths forming a slight curve, a carefully pleasant expression, if not quite a smile. My mother's hair, white since her thirties, forms a shiny halo. She is plumper than my father, already committed to his ascetic diet. A caption for this photo? Mature Americans, well-dressed, well-mannered, successful people who have come a long way to deserved rewards.

I turn to look at my father. Still asleep.

Finally I force my eyes to look up to the photograph that hangs above him: my mother at his eightieth birthday party, three weeks before she died. She is wearing a bold floral print that hangs loosely on her shoulders, showing the sudden loss of weight none of us had noticed. The flowers on her dress are too large, too bright, vaguely unpleasant, as cheap print fabrics always are. The only really fine dress she ever allowed herself to buy, with my father's rare encouragement, she wore at their golden wedding party. We buried her in it.

Next to the loud colors, her skin is pale ivory, her hair still a feathery white halo. Her reddened lips open in a gentle smile, not like the careful curve of the formal portrait, yet joyless, only too weak to be tense. Above the smile made for the camera, her eyes say the truth. Heavy-lidded and dull, eyes too weary even to weep. Her hands are clasped on her lap like those of an obedient child in an old-fashioned schoolroom.

I have a photograph of her actually taken in a schoolroom on graduation day fifty-five years ago. It is in her high school yearbook, the only keepsake I took when she died. She was eighteen. She had been working after school from the age of ten. As soon as the law allowed, her father yanked her out of school. For the past two years she had worked full time as the bookkeeper for a large firm, a rarity among the girls who left school at sixteen. At night, after work, she went to her teachers' homes to keep up with her class. She returned to

Redwood High School on graduation day, the first and only high school graduate among her family and *paisani*.

She stands out from every other girl in the yearbook because she has long hair; her father forbade her to cut it, made her wear it in the old-fashioned way, pinned up in dark, full waves around her high forehead. Her face is too thin. Her eyes are dark and intense, her nose a trifle too strong for prettiness. She looks older than eighteen, with her unsmiling mouth and her solemn, determined eyes. The caption under her picture reads

Lina Carlo

Talent: A Head for Figures

Secret Ambition: Tap Dancer

A few months after that picture was taken, she left home, not by plan but suddenly, impulsively. In the midst of a beating she broke away and ran. She ran in the only direction she could imagine, to my father's arms. "I'll take you home with me, Sweetheart." So they were married, and then she was pregnant, and the high school yearbook was buried in the bottom of her carved Chinese hope chest.

I wish I had told her that I don't blame her for wanting something more than the babies that came too soon. So did I, and my rebellion began an awkward juggling act, my chldren's needs and mine, that might have been no better than her angry sacrifice.

I wish I had told her that I built my rebellion on her anger, rebelling not really against her, but against bonds that held us both.

I wish I had told her that, free to choose, I moved toward my real life with what she gave me—her consistency, her passion, her jaw-clenched determination to stick to the job after it gets hard.

Would she have wanted to hear me say those words? She

117

might have been appalled. She probably wanted me to say only what I did, finally. As she lay comatose, I held her hand and put my mouth close to her ear, and repeated, "I love you, Mom. I'm here. I love you," over and over, because the nurse said, "the hearing is the last to go."

She could not move, but I knew she could hear. I knew because when my father bent over her and said, "I'll take you home with me, Sweetheart," a frown of weary exasperation flickered across her brow.

So. What Really Happened to the solemn, determined girl in the yearbook photo? Which woman is my mother? The exhausted, emaciated, sad woman on the wall beside my father? Or the one with him on the wall beside me?

I turn back again to the portrait of my parents. There must have been a reason why they posed for this portrait, gave copies to their daughters and grandchildren. They must have felt they had arrived at something worth commemorating.

Those were their good years. They closed the door on their shop and their long hours of work. They rediscovered old friends, ate and drank and danced with them in the last vestiges of Italian-American social clubs. They traveled, not only to the village of their birth but all over the United States, in the new Chevy that sits in the garage, still shiny and undented. They gambled in red plush Reno casinos, their monthly wickedness limited to twenty dollars lost in slot machines, and sometimes to jubilant winnings of even more. They built this house, cultivated their garden. Their family gathered on holidays, and if we brought them disappointments and conflicts, these were no worse than what their friends suffered from their children.

These are the years my father is living when he says, "We had everything." He has erased the last ten years, her failing body, his mind's descent into parody of his worst traits. Is there wisdom in his amnesia? Am I wrong to dwell on the suffering of her last years, distorting the shape of her life? Old age is more cruel than I ever imagined, uncovering buried defeats, desires, bitterness. But I must not deny the triumph of their middle years, the enormous distance they had come from the dirt floors of that feudal village. An entire life should not be judged by its worst days.

"What? Huh?" My father is startled awake by a shriek from the television. He turns, looks at me, and his mouth opens in a smile of sweet contentment. The smile holds for an instant, until his eyes focus. He sees that the woman beside him is not Lina. The smile drains away as he slowly remembers. He shakes his head. "I dozed off. What time is it?"

"About three. We'll go soon."

"Plenty of time."

"You'll want to shave and shower, maybe change clothes?" He starts to frown, shakes his head. To head off refusal, I change the subject. "And you wanted to call Flora."

"Flora?" He presses the armrests of his chair and uprights himself. "Let's turn off that noise!" While I am pushing myself upright, he gets up to turn off the television, grunting as he flexes his stiff legs. "Was I supposed to call Flora?" he shakes his head. "Better not. She gets awful mad when I call her. She said not to call anymore."

"No, Dad, that was me. I mean, no, I didn't say it either, but you thought I did. It was someone else, maybe. Anyway you wanted to tell Flora that Develia is moving in. Once that's settled, I'll take my ad out of the paper. In fact, I can call the newspaper while you're in the shower."

"Wait a minute, not so fast." he looks at me sternly. "Slow down for a minute, and just think. That woman . . . you don't know a thing about her. You know she's been married three or four times? The kind you have to watch. Oh, I can spot them a mile away, but you . . ." He points his finger at me. ". . . you always were so gullible, with all your college education."

I sit dumb, stunned, afraid to agree or disagree, unsure what effect my opinion might have on his. Finally I stammer, "But . . . but . . . you said . . . I thought . . ."

"I'm not going to argue about it. I may be old, but I'm not stupid. If she thinks she can take me for a sucker, she's got another think coming. No, I won't have her in this house." He rubs his cheek. "You think I need a shave? Shower too. Huh. Wouldn't hurt to look sharp for my test." He quick-steps to the hall door. I hear his feet tapping down the hall toward his bedroom.

"Hello?"

"Hi, Flora, it's me, Pat."

"Is it over?"

"No, we're getting ready to go. He's in the shower. I just had to tell somebody what . . ."

"Oh, God, what's he done now?"

"No, it's good news. About Develia. First of all, she was here."

"Today?"

"Right after noon. I think she came on purpose to meet me, to try to get me on her side."

"The bitch."

"You were right all along. She let slip that she had tried to get him to go to Reno and marry her."

"When?"

"I don't know. More than once, I would guess. Anyway,

after she left, I did what we agreed on. I said, "It's your decision." Guess what? He doesn't want her. Absolutely not. She's just after what she can get."

"He said that?"

"He did. One minute he was at me as usual, you know, he wanted 'that woman.' Then suddenly, she was trying to take him, I was the gullible one, but he wouldn't have her in his house."

"When he gets out of the shower, he'll start all over again, saying he wants her."

"I don't think so. This was different. He wasn't giving in and then reversing himself. He was . . . telling me off." I laugh but hear only silence. "Flora?"

She sighs. "As soon as we gave in, she wasn't what he wanted anymore. Maybe I should have given in a year ago."

"You couldn't take that chance. The only thing we could have done sooner was the Trust, and his doctor wouldn't have supported it at first, and . . . no, I think the whole melodrama had to go just the way it did."

"So he could play us off against her?"

"Apparently. This sounds terrible but . . . do you think he enjoys driving us crazy?"

"I think . . ." Flora pauses for another long silence. ". . . that is the only power he has left."

"Or will be when we're through with his driving test."

Suddenly Flora laughs. "She did us a favor!"

"Who, Develia?"

"Sure. If it hadn't been for her, we wouldn't have thought of the Trust, and look how much easier things are now that we have it."

"You want to call her up and thank her?"

Flora giggles again. "I don't think we have to go quite that far. Call me as soon as it's over. I'm going to make him

121

a 'present' of cab fare for wherever he wants to go. That might sweeten the pill."

"Good idea. Bye."

I hang up, then dial Joe and Mark's number. I'm late with my usual call to say hello to Mark, ask how he feels, share a joke, any joke. Today the joke will be the latest in the soap opera of Develia. Five rings, six. He could be in the garden. Joe tried to hire someone to help, but Mark balked. Not yet, not while he could still do anything, even a few minutes a day. In this passion and skill he is closer than any of us to my father, who has never addressed a word to him.

On the wall above the phone hangs a sheet of paper where I have printed frequently called numbers and emergency numbers in large, bold figures. My father prefers to scribble on scraps of paper he scatters on the shelf below the phone. Today there are three scraps with my number on them, two with Flora's, one for Barelli, the wine merchant, one of Develia's business cards. During our visits we clear the shelf of duplicates, including Develia's card (another always appears again within days, a sign of her persistent presence, like the footprint of an invisible predator). I will leave her card here this time, see what happens.

Too many rings. I break the connection and dial Joe's work number.

"Public Library, Reference."

"Is Joe Maretti there?"

"No, may I help you?"

"Will he be back soon?"

Hesitation. "He's not in today. Any message?"

"No message. Thanks." I break the connection and dial the number I know as well as I know the other two.

"Pacific Medical."

"Do you have a patient named Mark Lum? He would

have been admitted just today or possibly during the night."

"Room 927." The voice blurs into a buzz, just one ring before the phone is picked up."

"Hello."

"Hi, Joe, it's me."

"Hi, Mom."

"So what's doing." My voice is flat, casual, the tone I have learned from Joe. Like old soldiers in a long war, we are matter-of-fact, disciplined, low-key, saving energy for when it is needed.

"We came in about three o'clock this morning. I couldn't bring his fever down, and the abdominal distension has gotten worse. I wanted him here where he can be on oxygen."

"What does the doctor say?"

"She's starting some morphine, suggested I stay tonight." His voice is even more bland. "They're putting up a cot for me. I think I might take a little nap now."

"I'll come as soon as I can."

"No rush, but . . . yes, come today. I called you earlier but you weren't there."

"I'm at Grandpa's."

"Oh, right, it's the big day." His voice becomes fainter; he has turned away from the mouthpiece. "It's test-drive day for the ten-mile-an-hour terror of the road." A pause, then he laughs.

"Mark's awake?"

"Oh, sure. He says . . . wait a minute . . . Mark says don't go along on the test drive, or he's sure to outlive you." We laugh. Another discipline learned from Joe and Mark— laughing, as often as possible. There will be time later for tears.

"His test is at four. I'm not sure how long it will take. I should be starting back by five, five-thirty. Going against commute traffic, I can probably get back to the city by six-thirty."

"Good. After you see Mark, I'll take a break. His folks should be here by then."

"We'll go out for dinner."

"Right. Oh, and do me a favor. Call Amy? I've been too busy."

"Sure. See you about six-thirty. Give Mark a kiss for me."

I dial again.

"Legal Aid Society."

"Is Amy Maretti free? This is her mother."

"I think she's with a client . . . no, wait, I think she's free now. I'll put you through." A click, a few bars of Duke Ellington, another click.

"Hi, Mom? I thought you were at Grandpa's."

"I am. We're leaving in a few minutes for his test. Joe asked me to call you. Mark's back in the hospital. Want to meet us there about six-thirty?"

"Oh. I have a meeting at six. I guess I could get out of it if you think I should."

"I think you should. The doctor told Joe to stay tonight. I think that means we should . . ." Her sob interrupts me. I ignore it, pretend not to hear, backing off from contagion. "So I'll see you at Pacific Medical about six-thirty, and we'll take Joe out and get some food into him."

Amy laughs. "You're such an Italian mama. *Mangia, mangia!*"

As I hang up, my father appears in the doorway to the hall. He has pink, shaven cheeks, wears clean khaki pants and a fresh blue chambray shirt, both more baggy than the ones they replaced. He has added something to this habitual outfit. Around his neck, under the loose shirt collar, hangs a black leather thong, its ends passed through the silver medallion

124

cinched up to his throat. A souvenir of an old trip to Reno, a gesture toward formality, symbol of a tie. He is smiling anxiously, waiting for my approval.

"Dad, I won't be able to stay for dinner after all."

He winces as if I have slapped his face.

"I'm sorry, but Mark is back in the hospital, and . . ."

"Have I got anything to eat here?"

"Yes, there's the seafood I brought."

"Where?"

I point to the refrigerator. He shuffles over to it, opens it, peers in, nods, then lifts his eyes to the clock above the refrigerator. He looks at it for a moment, then asks, "What time is it?"

"About twenty to four."

"Time to go!" He hurries to the laundry room and puts on the shredded straw hat.

"Dad, maybe . . . do you have another hat?" At least let him lose this battle with some dignity intact.

He pulls off the straw, peers at it, shrugs, then nods and goes back to his bedroom.

Did he hear what I said about Mark? Did he interrupt out of pure anxiety for himself or to stop me from telling him? How much does he know or guess, forget or ignore? Mark's diagnosis came just after my mother died, too soon, we agreed, to add another shock by telling him, explaining what it meant, for Mark, for Joe. We would give him time, not hide anything, explain when he asked. He has never asked. If Mark is mentioned, he changes the subject.

He does know. The conviction comes over me with a flush of anger. He pushes aside the tragedy coming down on us while he wheedles, whines, manipulates, caring for nothing but his needs, his narrow interests, his petty comforts, to be served in his way. All right, all right. Take a deep breath.

It's better this way, better that he never asks. The less I say, the better I am able to keep my balance, to save energy for each problem in its own time and place, to live in the moment, as he does.

He appears wearing a gray felt fedora. "Is this better?"

"Much better. Don't forget your glasses."

"Where are my glasses?"

I point to the tray beside his recliner. He picks up the glasses and puts them into his shirt pocket, then turns to face me.

He stands there for a moment, an apprehensive grin twisting his mouth.

His grimace of sad defiance is exactly the expression he wears in a seventy-year-old photo in our old family album. Rows of scrappily-dressed children of miners, a curly-haired, blonde, round-faced boy of ten in overalls—my father in his fourth grade class, his first year in America. Whenever he looks at that photo he says, "You teach English to Mexicans and Chinamen? I'll tell them how you learn English, you get beat up every day on the way home from school till you speak without an accent, that's how you learn English!"

"What do you think? Do I look . . . very old?"

"You look just fine, Dad. Let's go."

He leads me through the back doorway, stops, turns the knob to make sure it is locked. I follow him along the path, past the gnarled rosemary bush scraping its metallic sweetness across our arms, past the gate held open in its branches.

"Wait, Dad," I call as he crosses the driveway. "We have to get the Chevy out of the garage."

"No, we'll take the pickup."

I shake my head. "Remember, the new battery needs to be installed."

"It'll only take a minute."

"We don't have time. Let's get the Chevy out, Dad."

"We could use your car."

"I don't think it's a good idea to take a test with an unfamiliar car." Why am I arguing with him? He'll never get as far as the driving test.

"Oh, we'll just go there in your car, then I'll use one of theirs."

"They don't provide test cars."

"Sure they do."

"No. Remember, I called them after you first told me that. They said . . ."

"They used to."

". . . they don't provide test cars and never did. Come on, Dad, we're wasting time. If we miss your appointment, your license is automatically cancelled." Or, with another appeal, they might reschedule his test, and I would have to go through this day all over again.

He unlocks the garage door and starts to slide it open. It is heavy and sticks, but he moves it easily, throwing his weight behind his push, a habitual leaning, just so. I come up behind him to do what I have rehearsed in my mind for days—snatch the keys out of the lock—but he is too quick for me, has them already in his hand.

I take a breath, then put out my hand, palm up. "I'll drive."

"No!" He turns on me in astonishment.

I keep my palm extended. I have rehearsed this gesture too. Flora agrees. My going with him to the test must not imply approval of his determination to drive. I speak the line

127

I have rehearsed to answer his objection. "Either I drive, or I'm not going." I cannot look at him as I make my quiet threat. My stomach churns with my shame.

"Well. Let me back it out. I haven't run it for a while. You have to know just how to start it."

"Okay."

I stand back as he goes into the dark garage. On the third try, the motor starts. I hear him gun the motor a few times. Then, slowly, out of the darkness appears the rear end of the silvery blue, long, fat car, a leftover from the days when even Chevys had grown rather grand. I push the garage door shut, then turn and blink at the chrome grill shimmering brightly in the sunshine. Flora's son has begun eyeing this car covetously. It stands midway between worthless old gas guzzler and mint-condition antique. As I approach the driver's side and open the door, my father hesitates, flashes a bitter look at me. Then he gets out and walks around the car to the passenger side.

I get in, gently touch the gas pedal, then test the brake pedal, my heart sinking as it sinks loosely, nearly to the floor before it engages. I reach for my seat belt, but, never used, it is stuck. Before releasing the emergency brake, I put my right hand on the automatic gearshift that takes up a wide space between our high bucket seats. I try to slide it into reverse, but can't budge it. He watches, lets me wiggle it for a minute, then says, in a soft, satisfied voice, "You have to push the little button on the side first. See? That's right. Now, don't forget to release your brake. Watch out, the traffic goes pretty fast on this street. Okay. No, wait! Okay, it's all clear. Go left. Left! Well, all right, if you want to go that way. Not too fast. The speed limit is twenty-five here, and there's an arterial up there. I mean the next corner, but this one is tricky too. Okay, it's clear. Watch out for that truck!"

We will never make it to the motor vehicle office. I will slam down the gas pedal, scream, spin the wheel in wild circles, smash into that pole! If he says one more word . . .

"Look at that!"

It is not another warning. He is pointing to the lemon tree in front of a house we are passing. The tree is huge, round and green, with hundreds of lemons hanging, big as my fist, gleaming golden balls.

"Isn't that something!" As we roll past, he slowly shakes his head in wonder.

"Yes. Beautiful." I am too surprised to say more. I can't remember such a spontaneous, emotional tribute to natural beauty ever coming from him before.

"We are so lucky."

Another surprise. I have to resist taking my eyes off the road to stare at him. I know I've never hear him call himself lucky.

"So lucky to live here. There's no place in the world like it. You know that?"

"You're right, Dad. We are lucky." I smile, and my tight gut loosens. I feel a surge of gratitude that he caused me to be born here, fed me, clothed me, sent me to school, never lifted a hand against me, nourished me as well as he could in his way. "It's a sort of miracle that our family made it all the way here."

"I was the first to leave Montana, you know. I was seventeen, been working three years, had a little change in my pocket. It was February, snow up to here. Winter was always the worst near the mines. I decided to get away, take the train to the coast, work up and down here for a while. I don't know what I expected, nothing like this. Those days, it was even better, more open land and trees and animals. People told me, but I never imagined . . . those days the train came right through the redwood forest. When I saw that, I . . . I'll never forget it. I looked up, up those redwoods and all at once I understood what people meant when they called a place God's Country. If there was a God, here was a sign of Him, this was holy ground. That's what I thought. I wrote to my folks right away. Pack and come. Just sell anything you have and buy your tickets. Don't wait for Pa to die in the mines like all the others. He'll get better here. This is the only place to live. Just come. No! Not that way, up here!"

He is directing me again, and he is right. He recognizes the sharp turn of the entrance into the crowded parking lot.

I park the car, hand him his keys, and we get out. He leads the way across the crowded parking lot. Out in this open space his quick, short steps look feeble. Hurrying, he covers ground slowly, blinking against the hot, low afternoon sun. We approach the office, a broad, low cube of brown glass bound together by strips of brown metal, a building as blank and hidden as if its walls were solid stone.

I push open the door to white brightness, open, cold space, broken by long lines of people. He stops abruptly as if blinded and frozen by the fluorescent lights and air conditioning. He turns to me. "What do we . . ."

I pull the letter from my bag and scan it quickly. "It doesn't say anything except to be here at four." I hand him the letter. "Take this to one of the people behind the counter and ask where you go. When he hesitates, I say, "I'm right behind you."

His eyes sweep the long twisting counter, moving slowly from one face to another. They stop at a woman a few years older than I, silver-blue hair in neat waves, face carefully painted white and rosy, neat print dress in a style unchanged for forty years. Another of those patient, courteous, accessible women I encounter while taking my father from one office to another, a species I am afraid is dying out. My father moves toward her. Maybe he remembers her as someone who had helped him before, or he sees that she has just come from a back room; there is no line in front of her.

Yes, she has helped him before. She remembers him. As he moves toward her, I see her smile clench into a grimace of irritation, even dread, braced for unpleasantness. Maybe she is the one who caught him cheating on the written test, or the one he accused of hitting him "in the eye" when he failed his vision test. Or maybe he has come to her over and over again, questioning, pleading, denying, arguing.

He shows the letter to her. She glances at it. Then, without speaking, she turns and points to the far end of the building, beyond all the counters and lines of people.

We cut through the lines, walking across the expanse of hard brightness. Through the brown window walls I see a dim, midnight view of the trees and cars outside. My father is breathing quick, shallow breaths. It seems to take us a very long time to make our way clear to the other end, to a dim alcove under a clock whose hands point to exactly four o'clock. In the alcove there are three chairs facing a door marked

EXAMINER'S OFFICE
PLEASE BE SEATED.

My father stands looking at the sign, then turns to me for guidance.

"I think we're supposed to sit down here and wait."

He sinks into a chair with a sigh of exhaustion. My knees feel a bit wobbly as I sit down next to him. Beside the door is a large window through which I can see the examiner's office, a long, narrow room. At the far end stands a desk with one chair on either side of it. Otherwise, the room is empty.

"What are we supposed to do?"

"I don't know, Dad. Just wait till someone comes, I guess.

131

For the third time he asks, "What time is it?"

"Ten after four."

"What are we waiting for?"

"I don't know. I'll try to find out." I stand up and step out of the alcove into the brightness of the main room. Lines of people stretch, undiminished, from the counter to the far glass walls, as if unmoving, unchanged. A woman comes from an office behind the counter. She is about forty, with black-dyed hair and green eyelids, wearing a wine-red suit and a bracelet jingling with dozens of keys—signs of authority?

"Miss?" I step up to the counter. "Pardon me!" She turns to me with a preoccupied, polite smile. I point to the alcove. "Can you tell me how long we have to wait?"

"You have an appointment?"

"My father." I take out the letter and hand it to her.

"Oh, yes. Sorry to keep you waiting. We're so busy today. The examiner isn't here yet. You go back and sit down and I'll see what I can find out." She turns toward the office behind the counter, taking the letter with her. I go back into the alcove and sink into the chair beside my father. This time my knees are definitely shaky, and the weakness is spreading upward, opening a cold hollow in my mid-section.

Was it John Brown who . . . yes, he stood on the scaffold while squads assembled and marched up and down and officers talked, until finally he asked if they would please hurry up and hang him.

"What did you find out?"

"The examiner's not here yet."

"How long are we supposed to wait for this joker?"

"Damned if I know, Dad."

"What time is it?"

"Four-fifteen."

But the woman in red returns almost immediately, jingling and smiling. "I called the city office. The examiner left an hour ago, but you know how traffic is this time of day. You're Mister . . ." She looks at the letter again. ". . . Mister Sancavei." She pronounces it correctly without hesitation, probably another Italian-American daughter.

He looks up at her as if he is getting ready to duck a blow. The cold hollow at my center has become a fist, clenching, then opening to extend icy fingers into my entrails.

"Well, Mister Sancavei, the examiner will be a little late, but while we're waiting, I can give you the written test."

"I already passed the written test!" His voice is suddenly defiant, strong.

The woman smiles blandly at him, through him. "It's required. See, it says so here in the letter." He takes the letter from her and studies it as if he has never seen it before, repeating under his breath that he has passed the written test. Then, silently, he stares at the letter, playing for time, no John Brown, he.

"We do the written test in this office." She points toward the window looking into the long, narrow room. She pulls off her bracelet; her keys jingle wildly. "Once you start the test, you can't leave the room, so if you want to go to the bathroom or anything . . ." My father shakes his head, stands, watches her put a key to the knob of the door. Then he turns to me and motions me to get up, follow him. How can I stand on legs that have turned to water? "No one can come in with you, sir, except me. I will sit at the desk with you. You can't leave until the test is over. No one else can enter."

I am limp with gratitude. I will not have to refuse to help him. He turns to her, opens his mouth, then closes it again and turns back to me with one more pleading look. I turn my hands up and shrug my helplessness while inside me an icy finger flicks upward, yes, somewhere into the area where my heart beats, flips it, sends it bouncing against my ribs. He turns away and follows the woman through the door, which she locks behind them.

I watch through the window as she leads him to the far end of the narrow room. She sits behind the desk and motions him to the chair facing her, his back to me. From a drawer she takes out a long sheet of paper and a pencil, hands them to him. Then she leans back in her chair, folds her hands in her lap, and sits watching him. He says something; she shakes her head. He sits still for a moment, then puts down the pencil. Has he given up already? No, he is fumbling with something on his shirt front . . . his pocket? His glasses, of course. He must be drawing the case from his pocket, opening it . . . yes, I can see him putting on his glasses, curling the ear pieces over his ears, bending his head over the paper on the desk, all like a film in slow motion.

A ridiculous movie image invades my mind, a scene from a terrible Biblical epic: Christians in the dungeon of a Roman arena, a tortured old man climbing up to peer through a window to watch his old wife torn apart by lions, saying, "We have shared a lifetime of happiness; I must share this with her too." My father probably feels that I have thrown him to these lions. At the moment, so do I, and without being able to say we have shared happiness, shared any victories before this defeat.

He lifts his head slightly, moves his hand, hesitates, then touches the pencil to the paper. He heaves his shoulders in a great sigh, then bends his head again over the paper.

I imagine him reading a question as he did with me last week. "Before you open the door on the traffic side of your parked car you should . . ." By the time his eyes reach "parked car," he forgets that the problem involves the opening of the door. He goes back to the beginning, opening the door, no, not on the curb, on the traffic side, you know, the side where the cars are coming. Now you have to choose the correct answer. Read the three choices: "Give a hand and arm signal for a left turn; Step on your brakes to flash your stop lights; Look around for bicycles and other vehicles." One of those three is the right answer. Choose the right one. What was the question? "Before you open the door . . ."

He moves the pencil to the paper, draws it back again, shakes his head, bends over the paper again, freezes for a full minute, then slowly lowers the pencil to make a mark.

I stand and walk to the end of the alcove, through the door marked WOMEN. I urinate, wash my hands, finger-brush my hair. But I am long past my days of killing time in rest rooms. There is no make-up to repair, no alternate female impersonation to consider or plan while looking in the mirror. This face is it, unmasked, uneven, weathered, cracked by lines that split wildly when I laugh. Strong, says Amy, meaning, I suspect, severe. Grave, says Joe. Yes, gravity, in every sense, does its work through the years, and when at rest, this face droops around the mouth, usually more somber than the thoughts behind it. Was it Orwell who said that by the age of fifty we have the face we deserve? Well, screw you, George.

When I realized that I might grow old without a mate, I tried to prepare myself for the loss of physical, sexual attractiveness. No problem. I was never comfortable with that game; the usual come-on seldom felt flattering, or even friendly, let alone loving. Love, I've found elsewhere, in larger, unexpected forms. But what about sex? What would I do when I lived within a still craving but unwanted body? I foresaw and feared endless possibilities for frustration and shame.

I needn't have worried. The fever that drove me into

ludicrous collisions from my teens through my forties has all but left me in my fifties. I trust this will be a lasting peace, not a ten-year truce erupting in some "Death in Venice" obsession. I see self-help books promising sex in old age, and I suppose they are published because they sell. (In this my father is more in tune with our times than I am.) Why would anyone want to reactivate that itch? I'm with Socrates, who celebrated release from that "cruel slave-master." Who gave me that quote? Oh, yes, my dear friend Walter, whose heart stopped in the midst of sex with a stranger. "What a way to go," our friends joked, but I knew it was not the way Walter wanted.

I push the door open, walk through the alcove with my eyes averted from the little window. Out in the main room, I see a drinking fountain, gulp some water, stand looking at the lines of people. I look from face to face, concluding nothing from the bored, worried, stupid, cunning, abject, mean, dissipated looks on them. Orwell was wrong. "There are other things than dissipation that thicken the features. Tears for example." Who said that? All these little scrappy quotes pop up in my idle mind. Why didn't I listen to my fifth grade teacher and memorize some good poetry? Then I'd have something fine like music to play in my mind during times like these.

I go back into the alcove, sit, watch my father through the window. He sits bent over with the pencil poised in mid-air, frozen in the same position as when I left my chair, still in the arena, circled by the encroaching, relentless lions.

It is not quite true to say my father and I shared nothing in our lives before this ordeal. For all the vague, indifferent distance he maintained between us, he deeply influenced me with a decision he made at my birth: he forbade baptism. Why? Because priests were hypocrites, because Catholics were drowned in superstition, because the Church demanded money and babies, because . . .

"True, *é vero*, but why not baptize the girls?" asked everyone from my dubious mother to my tearful grandmother, to all their *paisani*, who had kept only what was comforting and convenient in the old faith. Birth and and marriage and death still had to be marked. Why deny your family the comforting rituals, the happy celebrations? "Why make such a big thing of it?"

I don't know why these arguments failed. My father never talked about his adamant contempt for priests, for churches, for any expression of religious faith. In his contempt I sensed a feeling of deep injury, of being cheated, a grudge against a god denied. It is very like the attitude of my friends.

Every one of them made some painful rebellion against a religious orthodoxy handed down through family. Every one of them remains, in some deep place, isolated, lost, cut off from an abolished god. Each is encased in a shell of stubborn, hurt pride, like a defense against an old lover who might appear again, playing upon old feelings, old needs. Each of them continues a struggle I never had to fight. I never had to believe a dogma, then question, then deny, then continue lifelong resistance like theirs. My father fought (still fights?) that war for me.

I sang psalms, from plainchant to Stravinsky, before I thought about the "meaning" of the words. I inhaled and exhaled the vibrations of Bach's *Passions* without reservation, no careful distance to keep between aesthetics and faith. Music has been for me a total immersion baptism. Faith is no strain; some truth is imbedded somewhere in all scriptures. Everything means something. Music reminds me that all places—including churches and temples with all their sins—

are, like the redwood forest in my father's young eyes, holy ground. An easy faith? Say a bare beginning. But I might be still stranded in rebellion if my father had not rebelled for me. Especially during this past year, whenever an inferno of grief and fear and guilt seemed about to claim me, I renewed my baptism in a mass celebrated by Palestrina or Bach or Mozart or Beethoven or Schubert or Bruckner or Britten, or Messiaen, *lumen de lumine, qui tollis peccata mundi,* and I was washed clean, forgiven, reborn.

The woman reaches out and takes the test paper away from my father. She runs through it in a few seconds, her pencil jabbing here and there, flips it over, jabs again, puts it down, looks at him, then speaks. I cannot see my father's face, only his arm, raised, gesticulating. She speaks again, and his hand moves more excitedly, makes a fist that comes down on the desk. She looks at the test, speaks, and he shakes his head. He will not accept failure. He is telling her that he was driving before she was born, building and rebuilding automobiles before there were licenses, that he has never had an accident, except once when the Model-T turned over and his mother broke her arm, that was back in, let's see, twenty-eight on that old Santa Cruz mountain road that washed out when . . . the woman interrupts him, leaning forward, speaking slowly and vehemently. Now they are both talking at once. Now both are silent. She picks up the test paper, points to something. He leans over it. She speaks again, he raises his head, answers, she speaks, back and forth, on and on.

I look at the clock. After five.

Suddenly they both stand and begin to move toward me,

toward the door. My back is drenched with sweat. My hands are gripping the arm rests of my chair, but the rest of my body is limp, except inside where my guts go on churning and clenching then churning again. I push myself up out of the chair as they come through, keys jingling like a bell that announces them. My father's face is quite red, and his mouth is set. He does not look at me. He is taking off his glasses, fumbling at his pocket for the case. I blink my eyes, but my vision does not clear. I have only squeezed out the tears. Behind my glasses, no one will notice. If I do not raise my hand to wipe them away, they will dry on my cheek. No one will notice.

The woman leads us out into the big, light room. "Oh, there's Mr. Sawyer now." Across the room, at the doorway, a young man is being let in by a dark, boyish guard who locks the door after him. It is closing time; people are being let out, not in. The lines are short. "Just in time for his driving test."

"Driving test?"

"Yes, he passed the written test, but he has to . . ."

"He passed the written test? Did you say . . ."

She is nodding, looking away from me, waving my father's papers at the entering man. My father has turned away from me too, following the direction of her waving arm, moving toward the man she is waving at.

"May I see his test?"

"Oh, I have to keep it, give it to Mr. Sawyer, for our records." She flicks the test sheet past me quickly.

"Can you just tell me how many questions he answered?"

"Oh, he answered all twenty-five."

"How many did he answer correctly?"

"Uh . . . you mean in writing? Fourteen or fifteen."

"I don't understand. Aren't you allowed to miss only five or six?"

139

"That's right. But then we discussed his wrong answers, and he was able to pick up enough right answers."

"Pick up? What do you mean, pick up? You tell him his choice was wrong, and that narrows it down to only two possibilities, and then you "discuss" it until he gives the right answer? You consider that a valid test? For that you locked him in a room?"

"If he can show that he actually understood—you know some people have language problems and . . ."

"My father is literate in English, always took the standard English test."

"Well, sometimes older people are slow to . . ."

"And that slowing down may impair their judgement, their reactions, their ability to drive safely!"

"Well, that's up to Mr. Sawyer to decide, isn't it?" The edge in her voice is accompanied by a sharp jangle as she pushes her bracelet up her arm.

"You wouldn't believe the traffic," says the tall, blond-mustached young man, very young, younger than Joe. He takes the papers from the woman, who quickly disappears. He does not look at them. "You're Mister . . . uh . . ."

"Sancavei. Pete Sancavei," says my father, looking up at him.

"Okay, Mister . . . uh . . . let's go."

My father turns to me. "Come on."

"No one else in the car."

"But she's my daughter."

"No-one-else-in-the-car-this-is-your-final-test-any-other-appeal-can-only-be-made-in-a-court-of-law-you-understand-that?" He looks at his watch. "Let's go." He strides toward the door, my father scurrying across the room behind him.

For a while I just stand still, frozen. Not numb, stiff with rage. At the woman who turned the written test into a joke. But even more, at my father, this man who through week after week, hour after hour with Flora or me, could not

140

understand a test question no matter how we explained it. This man who could not remember the question by the time he reached the first answer. This man who cannot write a check or read his mail or follow the instructions on his washing machine or remember what he said a minute ago. This man who telephones his daughters morning, noon and night to cry out his helplessness or to recite fantasies he invents to fill the holes in his reality. This man managed to correctly answer fifteen questions. Alone. What else can this helpless, confused old man do when no one can be persuaded, blackmailed, or frightened into doing it for him?

A halo appears over my left eye, a beautiful, golden, glittering arc, electrified barbed wire shooting off sparks—first sign of migraine about to strike. My rage will punish only me. I rummage in my purse, praying that . . . yes, here is one dusty Cafergot pill at the bottom. Taken at once, it might abort the headache I cannot afford to have, not today, not tonight. I hurry to the drinking fountain, toss the pill to the back of my throat, bend over the fountain, suck up and hold a sufficient mouthful of water.

As I straighten up, swallowing, I see them at the door being let back in by the guard. The examiner points toward the far end of the counter, and my father goes that way. The examiner rushes in the opposite direction, looking at his watch, almost colliding with me. "Oh! Yes, he's picking up his temporary license and having his picture taken. He should get his permanent one in about a month."

"What?"

"His license." He looks at me, irritated, then looks again at his watch. "It'll be good for four years."

"Wait a minute. Are you telling me he passed the driving test?"

"Yes, yes." He glances sharply at me again as if to check whether I am deaf or just stupid.

"You weren't out there five minutes. You couldn't even have gotten out of the parking lot."

He doesn't answer, only looks toward the door, leans toward it, ready to be off at a run.

"Wait a minute," I insist. "Just because it's quitting time and you have a date . . ."

"He has a good driving record, no accidents."

"He *had* a good driving record. But that has nothing to do with how he functions now. Now. On the road. Why do you think those other three examiners, yes, three, did you read those papers? Why do you think they failed him? If you'd spent ten minutes with him in traffic . . . when we leave here, I'll drive or he'll get lost two miles from his house. Memory loss, slow reaction, tunnel vision . . . when he's driving he's out to lunch!"

He shrugs, shakes his head. "Then why did you bring him to appeal?"

"What do I have to do with it? Does my being here influence you? It's his test. Your authority. If my opinion means something, you should have asked me, and I'd have told you that . . ."

He suddenly throws up his hands and shakes his head, shoulders, his whole body, as if shaking off all his authority, powerless. "If I fail him, he'll go to court!"

"So?"

He backs away from me.

"Wait a minute! So what if he . . . wait, are you like the income tax auditors?"

He takes another backward step, looking at me as if I am crazy.

"My daughter says if you're audited and the IRS denies a deduction, you just keep arguing, appealing, and if they think you're willing to go all the way to court, they'll give in because it's not worth the trouble, it even counts against the examiner."

He blinks, keeps backing off, his mouth tightening.

"I just want to know! Is that what really happened?"

He is already out of range of my voice, has turned his back on me, hurrying to the door. The security guard, who has watched us without hearing our words, raises his eyebrows and smiles as he opens the door. The two young men shrug in unison, congratulating themselves on having endured and escaped another difficult old woman.

"Got my license!"

"Congratulations." Sarcasm is mean and stupid. Breathe. Be generous. "Yes, Dad, you did it. I really learned something from you today." I'm just not sure what.

I ease the car out of the parking space and turn toward the parking lot exit. I stop there and wait as the traffic streams by. I look at my watch. Five-thirty.

"This isn't a driver's license." He holds the slip of paper out to me. "But I thought they said I passed!"

"It's a temporary."

"No, it's just this little bit of paper."

"Read it, Dad."

"I haven't got my glasses on." He holds it out to me.

"Then put them on! I'm driving." The light changes and I cross the crowded boulevard.

He fumbles at his shirt pocket, drops the slip of paper, bends to retrieve it, bumps his head on the dash, moans, straightens his hat, sighs, takes out his glasses case, drops it, catches it in his lap, sighs, turns to look apprehensively at my face—which must be truly fierce. I give up. I am no match for him.

"It's a temporary license. To carry until you get your permanent license in the mail, with your picture and all on it. Meanwhile this one is legal. Put it in your wallet so you don't lose it."

He reaches to his back pocket, draws out his thick wallet, and slips the paper into it. He returns the wallet to his pocket, then leans back and sighs. "Four more years."

No comment.

"Got my license."

"Yes."

I take a deep breath, let it out slowly, and rearrange my thinking. He will be driving legally. His insurance will continue; if he hits anyone, he will covered. This is good news for Flora and me. We've done our best. We tried to get him off the road, but we have been overruled. We need not steal his car to make him obey the law. We need not humiliate him. Whatever happens will not be our fault. We will continue to drive him to the bank, the doctor. We will stop nagging him to go anywhere else. With any luck, he will make his trip to and from the supermarket without incident. Unless the brakes fail.

"Look, Dad, to celebrate, let me give you a present. Next week we'll take the pickup to a mechanic . . ."

"I can do my own . . ."

". . . and have it gone over completely."

"They charge you an arm and a leg to . . ."

"I'll pay for it, whatever it needs."

"Those guys don't know anything. I was working on cars before they . . ."

"Then, when the pickup is done, I'll take this car in. These brakes are awfully spongy and . . ."

"I just lost brake fluid, but that joker . . ."

"I'll pay for it all, okay, Dad? I'll feel better knowing

you're driving cars that are in good condition."

"I can do whatever . . ."

"I know you can do it, but why should you crawl under a car and catch cold on that concrete? I'll pay for everything, Dad. It's a gift. To celebrate four more years."

"Four more years," he echoes, nodding, almost smiling.

"Okay, so next week we'll take the pickup over to Andy's."

He shrugs his acceptance. We have a project for the next few weeks, something to do, something to talk about.

I pull up into his driveway. "I'm going to let you put it into the garage, Dad. I have to go now. I'm late. I'll see you Wednesday."

His face falls. "Aren't you staying for dinner?"

"I can't."

"Have I got anything to eat?"

"Fish. In the refrigerator. Just warm it up."

"How about just a glass of sherry, to celebrate?"

"I'm late, Dad."

"When you coming back?"

"Wednesday, as usual. School starts next week, so I have to come later. But I'll stay for dinner, I promise. Wednesday."

"I worry about you driving back on that freeway, all those crazy drivers. If anything happened to you because of me . . ."

I would be touched if I didn't know what was coming next.

"Why don't you stay overnight? There's plenty of room."

"I have to go to the hospital. Mark is . . ."

"Oh, yeah," he cuts me off abruptly. "Well, got my license! I think it's this little paper they gave me." He is reaching toward his shirt pocket, fingers fumbling. "Where is it? I lost it!"

"It's in your wallet."

"Oh, yeah." He leans forward, reaches toward his back pocket.

"Dad, I have to go. Look, why don't you go in and call Flora, tell her the good news. I'll see you Wednesday."

I get out of the car, a wild mischief bubbling up to my throat. Trying not to laugh, I start to shake. Flora will not believe him. She will think he is confabulating. She will ask to speak to me, and he will say I am gone, and she will think this is another confabulation and will wonder what in hell has happened to me.

My father has gotten out of his car and stands watching me cross the driveway to the curb. I open my car door, wave at him, get in, start the motor, smile to let out some of my silent laughter, breathe deeply to stop my shaking. I back into the driveway to turn my car around. He is still watching me. I wave once more through my side window.

Suddenly, his face contorts in panic. "Wait! Wait!" He rushes toward me, his short, quick steps taking him slowly around his car to the side of mine. He bends his frightened face to my window and gasps, "When you coming back?"